PREGNANCY OF REVENGE

BY

JACQUELINE BAIRD

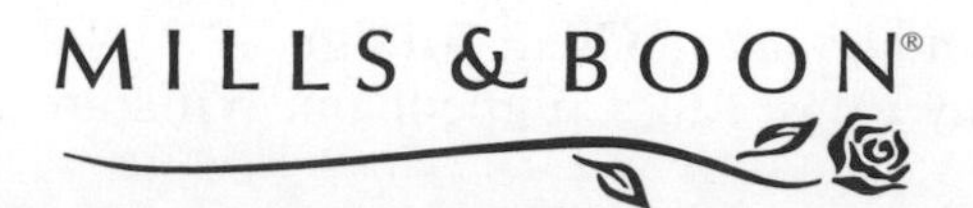

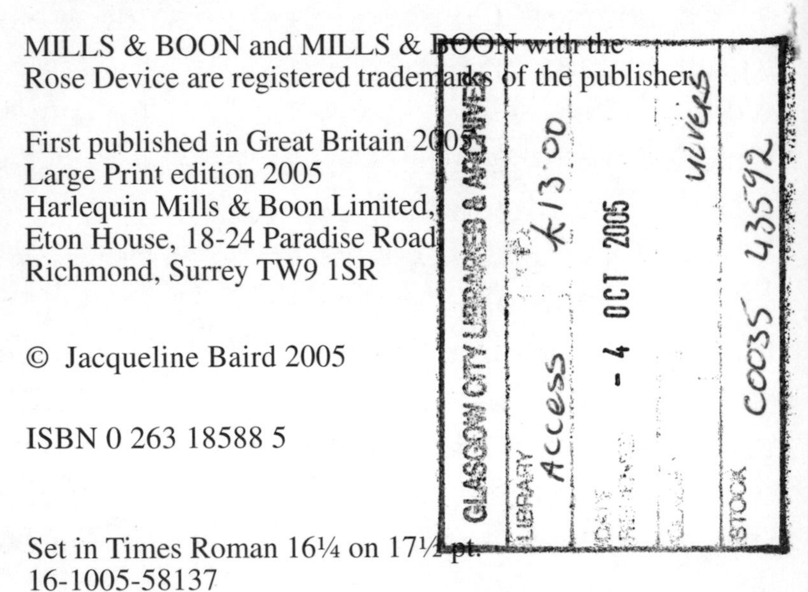

First published in Great Britain 2005
Large Print edition 2005
Harlequin Mills & Boon Limited,
Eton House, 18-24 Paradise Road
Richmond, Surrey TW9 1SR

ISBN 0 263 18588 5

Set in Times Roman 16¼ on 17½ pt.
16-1005-58137

Printed and bound in Great Britain
by Antony Rowe Ltd, Chippenham, Wiltshire

CHAPTER ONE

'EXCUSE me, Charlotte.' Ted Smyth, the owner of the prestigious London art gallery, gave the woman at his side a smile. 'But the prospective Italian purchaser of "The Waiting Woman" has just arrived. I must speak to him and get him to sign on the dotted line.'

'Of course.' Charlotte Summerville, Charlie to her friends and daughter of the artist whose works were being exhibited at the gallery, watched Ted vanish into the crowd and heaved a huge sigh of relief.

Alone at last. She glanced longingly at the exit. The bald old man who leered back at her must be the Italian purchaser Ted was chasing, she thought grimly. In fact, the whole event was grim to Charlie. Mingling with the top echelons of the London art world was not her scene, and she wondered how soon she could decently leave. Now would be good, she suddenly decided, and edged through the crowd towards the exit.

* * *

Jake d'Amato exited Ted Smyth's office having concluded a deal on a painting he had been determined to obtain from the moment he had discovered it existed. He had arrived in London a few hours ago from Italy, and gone directly to a business meeting. But as he'd checked into his hotel afterwards he had glanced over a stand of leaflets advertising forthcoming events, and the name Robert Summerville had caught his attention. He had unfolded the pamphlet announcing that an exhibition of the late artist's work was to open that evening, and an image of his foster-sister Anna had assaulted his vision. Filled with cold black rage, he had determined to prevent the showing.

A call to his lawyer had informed him that the artist's estate owned the copyright, and legally he could do nothing. Frustrated, he had realised he was too late to stop the portrait going on display, but he had made an immediate call to the gallery owner and reserved the painting.

By the time he had arrived at the gallery he had control of his temper. He knew Summerville had a young daughter, and the executors of his estate were entitled to sell the paintings for her benefit.

But Jake had been surprised to discover from Ted that the same daughter had opened the exhibition. What had really captured his interest was the fact she was not the young girl Anna had described to him as a spoilt little selfish brat, but a shrewd businesswoman. It had been her decision to sell the paintings. Robert Summerville was dead and beyond his reach, but a mature daughter put a very different complexion on the situation.

'So which lady is the artist's daughter?' Jake asked Ted with just the right amount of curiosity in his tone. 'I'd very much like to meet her and offer her my condolences on the sad loss of her father.'

And ask her what she intended doing with the exorbitant amount of money she was going to inherit, if the price of the picture he had just bought was anything to go by, Jake thought cynically. Not that he needed to ask—greed, plain and simple, had to be her motivation. Why else would she expose her late father's lovers to public scrutiny without having the grace to inform them first?

He hated Robert Summerville, although he had never met the man. But at least Summerville had had the decency to keep the paintings a secret. Not so his daughter. Jake could have forgiven a young girl for being influenced by the executors of the estate. In his experience most lawyers would sell their own grandmother if the price was right. But for an adult female to have so little respect for the women involved, and one in particular, Jake found disgusting.

His dark eyes narrowed. He could do nothing about the exposure the painting had already received. But he was going to put the woman down verbally and publicly, so neither she nor the assembled crowd would be left in any doubt as to his low opinion of her.

Charlotte Summerville deserved to be shown up for the avaricious bitch she was.

No trace of his true feelings showed on his hard dark face as he watched Ted look around and then point to a woman at the far side of the room.

'That's Charlotte, the blonde over there in black—standing by the portrait you've just bought, as it happens. Come on, I'll introduce you. I can remove the painting at the same time and have it sent to your home as we agreed.'

* * *

Musing on the vagaries of the artistic world, Charlie was totally unaware of the interest she had aroused in one particular male patron of the arts.

In life her father had been a modestly successful landscape artist, and it was only after his death that his private collection of nude portraits had come to light. Suddenly Robert Summerville was famous—or perhaps infamous was a better word, as it was rumoured he had been the lover of all the ladies he had painted.

It was probably true. Because, much as she'd loved her dad, there was no escaping the fact that he had been the most self-absorbed, self-indulgent man she had ever known. Tall, blond and handsome, with enough charm to woo a nun out of her habit, he had lived the life of the bohemian artist to the full. But he had never truly loved any woman.

No—she was being unfair. Her father had loved her, she knew. After her mother had died when she was eleven, her dad had insisted she spend a few weeks' holiday every year with him at his home in France. And he had left her everything he owned.

Charlie had known about one of the nude portraits, but she had discovered the rest when clearing out her dad's studio with Ted. It had come as something of a shock, but no great surprise. That was partly because, on her first visit to her father in France after the death of her mother, she had met Jess, his then lady friend, and liked her. But when Charlie had walked into his studio uninvited one day and found her dad naked with Jess, and saw the portrait he was working on, her dad had reacted with shame and fury. From then on he had always sent his current lover away when Charlie spent time with him. For a man of his morals to be so protective of his daughter was ironic, to say the least.

Ted had taken one look at the portraits and suggested arranging an exhibition. He'd advised Charlie to open it, to add human interest and help the sale of her father's work even more than his sudden death at the age of forty-six had done.

At first Charlie had flatly refused. She did not need the money. She had earned her own living for the past six years, when after the death of her grandfather she had taken over the running of the family hotel in the Lake District that had

'Charlotte, darling.' Ted's voice rang out loud and clear. 'I have someone here who wants to meet you.'

Charlie stiffened, cursing under her breath. Dwelling on the past, she had left it too late to escape. Reluctantly she lifted her head, resigned to wasting yet more time being polite to some wealthy fat old man who got off on looking at paintings of nude women. All in pursuit of the great god Mammon. Bare mammary glands were obviously a great money-spinner. Her lips curved up in a naughty smile at the thought.

'Allow me to introduce you to Jake d'Amato. He is a great admirer of your father's work, and has just bought this painting.'

Charlie's blue eyes, still lit with humour, met Ted's. 'Yes, of course.'

Privately she thought the man must be mad or blind. In her opinion her dad had been a much better landscape painter than portrait—apart from the last one; that did have character in the face. But she let nothing show on her face as, lifting her hand, she raised her eyes to the man at Ted's side.

There her gaze stuck as though hypnotised by the sheer physicality of the man. He wasn't the fat old man she had thought—anything but.

From his bronzed skin taut over high cheekbones to the straight nose and the firm mouth beneath, and finally to a hard, square jaw, the man was devastatingly attractive. Tall, something over six feet, and broad of shoulder, he exuded an aura of supreme confidence and masculine power that eclipsed every other man in the room. With his well-groomed black hair falling casually over his broad brow and his dark good looks he was clearly of Mediterranean descent. He was the most compellingly attractive man she had ever seen, and he was smiling down at her.

'Charlotte. I am delighted to meet you, and may I say how sorry I am at your sad loss?'

Somehow Charlie found her small hand enfolded in a strong male grasp, and he did not let it go. Not for him the brief handshake; and the piercing quality of the dark eyes that held hers was almost frightening in its intensity. She felt the power of his overwhelming masculinity like a blow to the heart, and her breath lodged in her throat.

A black brow quirked in amused enquiry as the silence lengthened and belatedly Charlie managed to respond with a mouth that had suddenly gone dry. 'Thank you, Mr d'Amato.'

'Oh, please, call me Jake. I do not want to stand on formality with you.' He lightly squeezed her hand. 'I too have recently lost a member of my family and I know exactly how you feel.'

Charlie fervently hoped not, because the warmth of his hand holding hers was sending an incredible surge of awareness through her whole body. But along with her purely physical reaction, she could not help being impressed by his sympathy. Her blood tingled and a curious spiralling excitement sizzled through her that made her even more tongue-tied, and she simply stared at him.

'But it must be a great consolation to you that your father has left you such a remarkable body of work.'

Body being the operative word. Charlie had the irreverent urge to giggle, and she could not prevent her lips parting in a broad smile.

'Yes, thank you,' she agreed, and tore her sparkling eyes from his to stare down at their joined hands. For heaven's sake, get a grip, she chided herself, and strove to control her erratically beating pulse. Finally she made a tentative effort to withdraw her hand from his, a responsive quiver lancing through her as he tightened his grip. In that moment she knew she would happily have held onto the man for ever, so fierce was her response to Jake d'Amato.

Jake noted her brilliant smile and it only added to his anger, but he let nothing show on his impressive features. 'It is my pleasure,' he said softly, and, bending his dark head, he pressed a swift kiss on the back of her hand, before finally releasing it. 'It is an honour to meet you. And now, please, you must give me your honest opinion on the painting I have purchased.' Placing a guiding hand at her waist, he turned her back to look at the portrait. 'Lovely, don't you agree?' Jake was determined to make her look at Anna's face—a woman she had insulted in life, but was happy to exploit after death.

The sound of Jake's deep, melodious voice sent another responsive quiver through Charlie, and his hand on her waist and the warmth of his great body seemed to envelop her. For the first time in her life she experienced the bone-melting awareness at the touch of a man, a sensation that overwhelmed her, and she knew with a feminine instinct as old as time that this man could be her destiny.

Charlie frowned. She wasn't given to flights of fantasy and it scared her, plus her intense awareness of him was tempered by the distaste she felt that he had bought the nude. Gathering together the shreds of her control, she said, 'Lovely, yes,' then added dryly, 'if you have a penchant for pictures of naked ladies.'

'You show me a man who does not, Charlotte, and I will show you a liar,' he said teasingly, his heavy lidded eyes sweeping over her beautiful face and lower to linger on the provocative thrust of her breasts. 'Though I must admit, I much prefer the live variety.' The brown eyes darkened, an unmistakable message in their depths, leaving Charlie more flustered than ever.

She could not believe it. Jake d'Amato was flirting with her. She didn't know how to respond so she simply smiled like some idiot teenager. She felt her nipples harden beneath the lace of her bra, and, hopelessly embarrassed, she blushed scarlet and was lost for words yet again.

Jake d'Amato stilled. The sexual attraction visible in her brilliant blue eyes plus the invitation in the tight nipples starkly outlined beneath the fabric of her dress had an unexpected effect on his powerful body. It had been a long time since a woman had so instantly aroused him. That it should be this woman would have shocked him rigid—if he had not been rigid already for a much more basic reason.

He did not like it. He had had every intention of putting her down in public. Revealing her as the selfish, money-grubbing parasite she was, and leaving. But suddenly that scenario no longer held such great appeal. Instead he found himself imagining what her lush lips would taste like—the high, firm breasts in his hands, in his mouth…and the only place he wanted to put her down was naked on a bed under him.

He must be going crazy. The Summerville family were responsible for the untimely death of Anna Lasio, and for the grief of her parents. Embarrassing Charlotte was nothing compared to the turmoil the Summervilles had caused in what was the closest thing to a family Jake possessed. Given that Charlotte Summerville was not the young girl he had been led to believe, but a mature woman who should know better, a much more satisfactory course of action sprang to mind.

He was here on business, with meetings lined up over the next fortnight. For once in his life combining business with pleasure held great appeal. Without conceit, he knew he was a good lover and it would be interesting to slowly seduce the lovely Charlotte until she was desperate to share his bed, as her father had done his foster-sister…

Turning on the charm, he murmured softly, 'Ah, I see I have embarrassed you, Charlotte.' His dark eyes narrowed on her face. 'You think I am some old lecher who spends his day ogling naked women, perhaps?' he prompted, and noted the deepening flush in her pale cheeks with amusement. It was a long time since he had seen a woman blush and Charlotte Summerville did it beautifully. She played the innocent to perfection, even though he was sure she was anything but.

'Let me set your mind at rest, Charlotte. I am a businessman first and foremost, and when I see a good deal I snap it up, whether it be a company or art. The painting is an investment. I do not wish to sound callous, but you, who sanctioned the exhibition, must be well aware work by a dead artist is much more marketable than that by a living one.'

The ease with which he had read her thoughts was scary. But Charlie knew his cynical assessment was correct. 'Yes,' she murmured, finally finding her voice.

'And let me reassure you…' his deep voice thickened as he turned back to the painting '…this is the only nude I want to own. I believe it is your father's best and last.'

Following the line of his gaze, Charlie looked once more at the picture, in which her father had captured the mood of the woman perfectly.

'Yes, she is beautiful,' she agreed again. But, though it might be his best, she knew it wasn't his last. There was a half-finished portrait in her possession of a red-headed woman. Determined to try and match his sophistication, she looked up at Jake. 'But not, I think, his last,' she said archly, and was about to tell him of Robert's last affair in what she hoped was a sophisticated attempt to keep his interest. But her effort was wasted; he wasn't listening. She saw the glazed look in his dark eyes, and reality hit her like a slap in the face. The man was transfixed by the portrait.

But then, he had just paid a hefty amount of money for the picture—why wouldn't he be fascinated? she told herself firmly. What was she thinking of, trying to impress a man she had just met? A man, moreover, who was captivated by the portrait of a luscious brunette. Where did that leave her, a very average blonde? Precisely nowhere, and she castigated herself for being a fool.

Her first assessment had been right before she'd ever seen Jake d'Amato. He was certainly no fat old man. The very opposite—a more striking male would be hard to find. But as for the rest, she had been correct. He was wealthy—it was evident in the supreme confidence he displayed, and in every line of the designer suit right down to the handmade shoes, never mind the fact he had bought the painting. But that aside, she told herself firmly if a little regretfully, he was also the type of guy who got off on looking at pictures of nude women.

Not her sort of man at all. She had been here far too long and it was scrambling her brain. She tightened her grip on her clutch bag and with a swift sidestep put some space between them.

'Well, I wish you joy of your purchase, Mr d'Amato. Nice to meet you, but now I must be leaving.' And, spinning on her heel, she dived headlong into the crowd before she made a bigger fool of herself than she already had.

Safely in the ladies' cloakroom, she studied her reflection in the mirror. Her face was flushed, her blue eyes unusually bright. She could not believe a man who was obviously from the same mould as her father could have such a startling effect on her, and it scared her witless. She had loved her dad, but only a complete idiot would willingly get entangled with a philanderer of the same ilk.

The only reason Charlotte existed was because Robert Summerville, nineteen and studying art, had got her mother pregnant, and her parents had insisted they marry. It was probably the only time in his life Robert had been coerced into anything. When he had graduated two years later he had left wife and daughter with the maternal grandparents in the Lake District and gone to find his 'true artist's soul'. Charlie and her mother hadn't seen him for three years, and only then to obtain the inevitable divorce.

Charlie suddenly thought it was quite possible Jake d'Amato was also a married man, and she had been so overwhelmed by his effect on her she had behaved like a fool. How embarrassing was that? She needed to get back to her own world, and quick. A taxi back to the apartment her friend Dave had lent her, a simple dinner and an early night were what she needed, not swooning over some man. Straightening her shoulders, she walked out of the cloakroom, and hastily left the building.

She stood on the edge of the pavement and glanced up and down the street. Not a taxi in sight. 'Damn it to hell,' she muttered.

'Now is that any way for a lady to talk? Shame on you, Charlotte,' a deep, dark voice drawled mockingly.

Charlie spun around, and found herself only inches away from a large male body. 'Mr d'Amato,' she said coolly, but she could do nothing about the surge of colour in her cheeks.

'Jake,' he corrected. 'Now what seems to be your problem, Charlotta? Maybe I can help.'

The accented way he said her name was enough to give her goose bumps. 'Most people call me Charlie, and I am trying to get a taxi back to my flat.'

'Charlie is no name for a beautiful woman and I refuse to use it,' he declared firmly. 'As for the taxi, that is no problem.' The smile accompanying his words held such devastating charm Charlie could not help smiling back. 'My car is here.' He gestured with one hand to the sleek navy blue saloon parked on double yellow lines about ten yards away. 'I'll take you wherever you want to go.'

'Oh, no, I couldn't possibly—'

'Preferably to dinner, and of course you can.'

Five minutes later she was seated in the passenger seat of a luxury car and Jake was in the driving seat, having ascertained she'd intended to eat alone, and bulldozed her into dining with him at a well-known London restaurant.

'Do you always get your own way?' Charlie asked dryly.

Jake turned slightly, his thigh brushing hers in the process. 'No, not always,' he said seriously, his dark eyes capturing hers. Reaching out, he clasped her small chin between his thumb and finger and tilted her face towards him. 'But when it is something or someone I truly want, I always succeed.'

Charlie swallowed hard and sought a witty comeback, but words failed her as his hands dropped to curve around her shoulders. He made no attempt to pull her into his arms. He didn't need to. His mouth covered hers and he coaxed her lips to part to the gentle invasion of his tongue. The steadily increasing passion of his kiss ignited a slow burning sensation deep down in her belly that was entirely new to her. Suddenly Charlie wanted him with a hunger that shocked even as it thrilled her, and instinctively her hands lifted to his broad shoulders, but she didn't reach them.

'*Dio mio!*' Jake exclaimed shakily, and, grasping her hands, he pulled back and pressed them to her sides. His heavy-lidded dark eyes swept over her dazed face, and lingered on her softly swollen lips.

'You are some woman,' he commented, and for a moment Charlie thought there was anger in the dark eyes that stared down at her. Then he pressed a brief kiss on the tip of her nose and added, 'I promised you dinner, the rest must wait.' He slanted her a wickedly seductive smile, before starting the car and driving off.

Charlie didn't say a word. She could hardly believe what had happened; it was so unlike her. Where had her common sense, the steely nerve she was noted for, gone? Banished into oblivion by one kiss. Her entire body thrummed with a strange excitement and she had never in her wildest dreams believed a man could make her feel so wonderfully, vibrantly alive. But what was even more unbelievable was that Jake seemed to be as captivated by her as she was with him. She had felt it in the pounding of his heart, his shaken reaction when he had ended the kiss.

Suddenly the dinner she had tried to refuse held great appeal.

CHAPTER TWO

IT WAS an exclusive French restaurant and at first glance appeared to be full, but within seconds of them entering the head waiter was at Jake's side, and declaring it was a great pleasure to see him again, and his charming companion. His shrewd eyes flashed an appreciative glance over Charlie as he bowed courteously and led them to a small table set for two in an intimate corner of the room.

She looked around the dining room, her blue eyes widening in awe as she recognised a couple of politicians and a few famous faces from television. 'You must have friends in high places,' she said, grinning across the table at Jake. 'I read an article about this restaurant in a Sunday supplement. But it's even better than I imagined, though I never thought I would ever eat here.' Eyes shining, she leant forward slightly. 'Apparently one has to book months in advance.'

'Obviously not in my case,' Jake said arrogantly as the waiter arrived with the menus.

Disconcerted by his cool reply, Charlotte felt her smile fade as she realised her mistake. He was a big man and every inch the dominant male. Add wealth and sophistication, and it would take a very brave man or a fool to turn him down. As for women—she only had to recall how easily he had overcome her objections to dining with him to know the woman probably wasn't born who could say *no* to him.

She gratefully accepted the menu from the waiter and buried her head in it, telling herself to get a grip. Instead of spouting off like some overenthusiastic teenager, she would show Jake d'Amato she could be as sophisticated as any woman.

'What would you like to eat? I am going to have the hot smoked salmon followed by the steak. How about you? The same?'

She placed the menu on the table and lifted her head. 'No, Jake,' she said coolly, before turning to the waiter and asking him in perfect French what he recommended. A lively debate ensued on the relative merit of the red sea bass or the chef's special stuffed trout. Finally Charlie gave her order for a starter of seasonal spring salad followed by the bass to a now beaming waiter, with a brilliant smile of her own.

'So, Charlotte,' Jake commented mockingly as the waiter departed. 'You are a woman of many talents, it would seem.'

Charlie turned sparkling eyes to the man seated opposite. 'Well, I'm not an idiot.' She smiled, her confidence restored.

'No, but, French aside, you did turn the poor waiter into a drooling idiot.' His eyes flashed with a hint of some dark emotion, then softened perceptibly as his gaze roamed down to the soft curve of her breasts. 'Though I can't say I blame him,' he added huskily.

She felt a flush of heat creep from her stomach to cover her whole body at his sensuous gaze, and she had to take a deep breath before she could respond steadily. 'Thank you for the compliment.'

'My pleasure, I assure you.'

Out of nowhere the thought of Jake at her pleasure deepened Charlie's colour, and she frowned. In the sexual stakes she was not in his league, and she wondered what she was letting herself in for.

Jake reached out to cover her slender hand resting on the table with his own. For some reason the reservation in her eyes bothered him. 'Charlotte, don't look so serious,' he said softly. Entwining his fingers with hers, he lifted her hand and pressed a tiny row of kisses across her knuckles. 'Please, relax and enjoy your meal, and let us see if we can get to know each other a little better. We can become friends—can we not?'

Friends? With every nerve in her body quivering at his casual touch, Charlie doubted she could ever be just *friends* with such a supreme specimen of the male sex as Jake. But it was a start.

'Friends. Yes.' Striving to appear cool, she continued conversationally, 'So, tell me, why the name Jake? It doesn't sound very Italian.'

'My mother was engaged to an engineer in the US Navy. She gave me his Christian name because he died in an accident at sea before she could give me his surname.'

'That is so sad.' Her eyes softened on his. 'Your mother must have been devastated, losing her fiancé like that.'

'Strange,' Jake said with an odd note in his voice. 'Most people respond with embarrassed silence or embarrassed laughter and a quip like, "I always knew you were a bastard." But you are obviously romantic at heart.' The fingers entwined with hers tightened slightly. 'And you are right. My mother was devastated. She never looked at another man to her dying day. Except me, of course, whom she adored,' he added with a soft chuckle, his dark eyes smiling warmly into hers.

'I'm not surprised.' Charlie grinned, relieved her casual query about his name had not embarrassed him. In fact, suddenly the atmosphere between them seemed much more relaxed. Maybe friendship with Jake was not so impossible after all, she thought happily. Though she wasn't sure she agreed that she was a romantic. She had always considered herself the most realistic of women. But then that was before she had met him…

'A compliment. I am flattered.' Jake grinned back.

'I didn't mean you. Well, maybe I did,' she added with a chuckle. 'But really I was referring to your mother. Having committed to getting married, she must have been as distraught at his death as any widow.'

'In my mother's case, yes, but that is very rare.' He leant back in his chair but still retained his grasp on her hand. 'In my experience, plenty of women see an engagement as simply a way of getting money out of a man.'

His cynical attitude appalled her. 'In your experience? You were engaged?'

'I was, once, when I was twenty-three and naive. I bought the ring, gave her money for the wedding, the whole nine yards.'

'And then you left her, I expect.' Charlie pinned on a smile as it struck her again that he might be married, and she hadn't asked—a glaring omission on her part, which she immediately rectified. 'Or else you're married.'

For a moment Jake looked astonished, then he laughed, but the humour didn't reach his eyes. 'How like a woman to blame the man.' His cool dark gaze held hers. 'But you are wrong. My fiancée left me, and spent the money on something else. So, no, I am not married, nor ever likely to be. It is not an institution I believe in.'

Feeling foolish, Charlie realised appearance could be deceptive. She could not imagine any woman turning Jake down, but she had been wrong, and that long-ago rejection must have hurt. Her soft heart went out to him. 'I'm sorry.'

'Don't be. I am not. But enough about me. Tell me how you learned to speak fluent French—and do you speak any other language?'

'No, just French.' She accepted his change of subject. Obviously it still hurt him to talk about his ex-fiancée, and it made him seem more human somehow. 'I learned French at school, but I became fluent mainly because from the age of eleven I used to spend a few weeks' holiday every year with my father at his home in France. Not so often in recent years, but I did stay with him last year, a little while before he died.'

'Ah, yes, your father. I should have guessed.' He dropped her hand, and a shadow seemed to pass over his face. Charlie wondered what she had said to cause it—or perhaps he was still thinking of his ex-fiancée? Then the wine waiter arrived with a bottle of Cristal champagne and filled two glasses before placing the bottle in the champagne cooler and leaving, and she banished the dark moment to the back of her mind.

'To us and the start of a long friendship,' Jake said, raising his glass, and Charlie reciprocated, her blue eyes shining into his as another waiter arrived with their food.

'So tell me, have you any other family?' Jake asked casually as they both tucked into their first course.

'My mother died when I was eleven, my grandmother when I was seventeen and my grandfather three years later. My father was an orphan, so I'm alone in the world now he's died.'

'With a father like yours, can you be certain of that?' Jake queried sardonically.

'Yes, I'm certain.' She glanced up, surprised by his cynical question, and thought she saw a bitter look in the dark eyes, but she must have been mistaken, as the next moment he grinned.

'Ah, another illusion bites the dust. I should have known the exploits of your father were more fiction than fact—probably circulated to increase the price of his work.'

'Well, I don't know about that,' Charlie murmured, pushing her empty plate away. There was something in the tone of his seemingly jocular comment that struck a discordant note and made her wary. Plus she was not comfortable talking about her father or about money.

flat while I am in London.' She rattled off the address in what she hoped was a cool voice.

'Nice location,' Jake said, his teeth clenching as he changed gear with less than his usual fluency. That left him no longer in any doubt there was a man in her life—a wealthy man, it would seem, if he owned an apartment in that area. It wasn't surprising; it only confirmed what he already suspected. Like father, like daughter. A woman like Charlotte was never going to be without a man for long, and the thought did nothing for his temper.

'But perhaps you would prefer a nightcap at my hotel before I take you home?' His original intention had been to move slowly, hoping to enthral her, the way her father had Anna. But now his only intention was to get her into his bed as soon as humanly possible, and keep her there until the memory of any other man was wiped from her mind. And at the same time cure his own irrational need for a woman whom by nature he should despise.

Colour swept Charlie's face. Was that the equivalent of, 'Your place or mine?' Whichever, she wanted to cry, *Yes!*—and it shook her to feel so vulnerable. She was hopelessly out of her depth and sinking fast. She had never met a man like Jake before.

Charlie had grown up in a home full of adults, and she had to some extent been left to run wild around the mountains and crags of her beloved Lakes. Her hobbies were sailing and rock climbing. She was a member of the local rescue team, and also of the International Rapid Rescue Team. With a good manager to run the hotel on a day-to-day basis, Charlie took care of the accounts and it worked out well. She kept her gear packed at all times at home, and simply postponed the paperwork when she was needed elsewhere.

She had recently returned from a trip to Turkey, where she had helped in an earthquake recovery, and gone straight into the hectic Easter holiday at the hotel. The two weeks she was spending in London were at the suggestion of Dave, her team leader. He thought that with the recent death of her father and running two jobs, she needed a complete change. Time to take an ordinary holiday, instead of being at the beck and call of other people all the time.

Charlie had agreed. She had visited hot spots all over the world, but now she was taking the chance to visit some of the highlights of her own capital city, something she had never done before.

As for men, she knew plenty on a professional level, but they all treated her as one of the boys, which was how she liked it. Glancing at Jake's perfectly chiselled profile, she realised that never in a million years could she think of him as one of the boys. In fact, she had trouble thinking at all around him.

The car came to a smooth stop, and Jake turned slightly in his seat, his black eyes gleaming with intent, capturing hers. 'So what is it to be—a nightcap? This is my hotel.'

She knew what he was offering, and it wasn't just a drink. The air in the close confines of the car positively crackled with sexual tension as he waited for her answer and suddenly Charlie was afraid. She tore her gaze from his and glanced out of the window. It was a very plush hotel, one of the best in the city, and she knew she couldn't do it…not yet.

'I think I have had enough to drink,' she said carefully, 'Thank you all the same.'

His dark eyes narrowed slightly, and she wondered if he was angry. But as she watched he shrugged his broad shoulders. 'Your decision.' Dropping a brief kiss on her brow, he turned and started the car before adding, 'I will pick you up for lunch tomorrow at twelve,' his attention on the road ahead. 'And we can move on from there.'

'Can we indeed?' she shot back. 'It would be nice to be asked instead of told.' But there was no bite to her words; secretly, she was relieved her attack of maidenly modesty had not ruined her chance with him after all. 'I'm here on holiday, following the tourist trail, and I intend to visit the British Museum tomorrow.'

Jake's every masculine instinct had been screaming out at him to persuade her into his bed, but the almost frightened look in her blue eyes had disconcerted him. She might be selfish and money-grubbing in her love affairs—in his experience, most women were—but it didn't necessarily follow she was promiscuous. Jake was very choosy himself. He preferred to pick his lovers with care and his affairs were always as discreet as he could make them, given his high profile in the international business world.

The only reason he was without a lover at the moment was, ironically enough, because of Charlotte's father. His death had created a set of circumstances that had kept Jake at home in Italy and caused him to neglect his last lover,

Melissa, a New York model, who had therefore moved on to another wealthy man.

It hadn't surprised him. Melissa had been a high-maintenance lady, he thought cynically as he stopped the car outside the apartment block, and slipped out to open the passenger door.

'Come on, Charlotte, I will see you inside.' He reached for her hand. 'And there I promise to leave you until tomorrow,' he reassured her with a dry smile. 'And before you argue—' he placed a finger over her lips '—we will do both. Lunch and the museum.' Fingers entwined, he walked her to the lift. Again he registered the wariness in her incredible eyes, and grinned. Little did she know she was in no more danger from him tonight. He drew the line at making love to her in a bed she had shared with another man. 'Until tomorrow.' He kissed her brow and left.

CHAPTER THREE

JAKE D'AMATO prowled around the enormous hotel suite. He was too frustrated to sleep, and it was all the fault of a particular blue-eyed blonde. Not quite all, he allowed—the painting of Anna played heavily on his mind as well.

It had taken all of his considerable powers of self-control to stand in that damned gallery and stare at the portrait, which, as the purchaser, had been expected of him. Anna was the nearest thing he had ever had to a sister and it had seemed almost incestuous to see her exposed in such a way.

As for the title, 'The Waiting Woman'—how apt, he thought grimly. She had waited and hoped for two years for Robert Summerville to marry her. A deep, dark frown marred his austere face as the memories flooded back. Jake had been twelve when Anna was born, and to his foster-parents her birth had seemed like a miracle. Jake had adored the new baby, and had watched her grow into a delightful little girl by the time he had left his foster home at eighteen.

He should have kept a closer eye on her. But after university he had been totally involved in his work as an engineer and building his own business. He had not had much time to visit his foster-family, mainly birthdays and holidays, but when he had Anna had always seemed fine. And as the Lasios had never appeared to have any worries about her, neither had Jake.

When Anna had turned twenty-one, Jake, then the head of the vast d'Amato International corporation, had thrown a lavish party on board his yacht for her birthday. Anna had seemed to be a happy, well-adjusted young woman, full of enthusiasm for her fledgling career as a graphic artist. Satisfied she was okay, Jake had carried on his own very busy life and respected that, as an adult, Anna was entitled to do the same.

But not any more.

Rage and regret welled up inside him. How could she have had an affair with, and posed naked for, a man who was old enough to be her father? How could she have driven when hopelessly drunk and killed herself? How could she have let a man do that to her?

There was no answer, and the burden of his own guilt had weighed heavily on his mind since Anna's death. He had lived with Anna from the moment she was born until she was six and with hindsight he knew he should have done much more to protect her.

He had known about her relationship with Summerville. She had told him over one of their infrequent lunches in Nice two years ago. At that time she had still been working and living in an apartment Jake had bought for her, and although Jake had never heard of the man, he had not queried her choice, because she had so obviously been happy, and confident it was only a matter of time before they married.

But now, remembering how appalled he had been when Anna had turned up at his home in Genoa five months ago, he bitterly regretted not investigating Summerville as soon as he'd heard the name.

Looking a shadow of her former self, Anna had cried on his shoulder and told him the whole sorry story of the affair. How she had given up her job and had been living with the man for over a year, but Robert had sent her away three months before he'd died, all because of his daughter.

He had explained she was his only child and had been spoilt by her mother. She was a bit insecure and very possessive of him, and flatly refused to meet Anna. He didn't want to upset his daughter, so Anna had to leave while she was in residence. But he had assured Anna it would only be for a few weeks. In other words, to quote Anna, 'Robert's daughter was a selfish little spoilt brat.' Anna had not even heard of his death in time to attend the funeral. For himself, after hearing the tale, if the man had not been dead already, Jake would have quite happily killed him.

Anna's tragic death a few weeks after their last meeting had gutted him, and it didn't help that the man who in Jake's mind was indirectly responsible was already six feet under and out of his reach. As for Anna's parents, they were crippled with grief.

Jake had spent the past three months simply being there for his foster-parents, his work for once taking second place.

This was his first trip abroad since her death, and catching sight of that catalogue in Reception had ignited his fury all over again. But at least he now knew the painting was safely on its way to his home in Italy. He was still angry he had been unable to prevent its showing, but, as he intended to destroy the painting, with a bit of luck Anna's parents need never know it had ever existed. It was the least he could do for them.

Jake considered himself a modern, sophisticated man of the world. He enjoyed women and was rarely without a lover. Over the years he had had several affairs, and at least two of the women, as models, had been displayed naked on countless magazine covers. It hadn't bothered him at all. Yet he saw nothing paradoxical in his reaction to the public exposure of Anna.

But what he did see after meeting the lovely Charlotte was a way to get revenge on the family that had brought about her death…and thoroughly enjoy doing so.

Spinning on his heel, he headed for the bathroom, and a cold shower. His last for some time, he reckoned, a predatory smile curving his firm mouth.

Charlie took one last look at her reflection in the mirrored door of the wardrobe. Slim-fitting grey trousers traced her long legs, and with them she had teamed a soft pink cashmere sweater. A heavy chain belt that fastened with a large clasp was slung low around her hips. A grey hide purse and matching loafers completed her outfit. Comfortably casual, she told herself, but in reality she hadn't much choice: the only dress she had with her was the one she'd worn last night and the rest of her holiday clothes consisted of trousers and casual tops. She tweaked a stray tendril of hair behind her ear, and wondered again if she should pin it up. As it was it fell in loose curls to her shoulders. No, you look good, girl, she decided with a broad grin.

Last night, tossing and turning in bed, unable to sleep for thinking about Jake, replaying in her mind his every kiss and touch, her body aching for him, she had reached a momentous decision. Given the chance, she was going to pursue her relationship with Jake. He had said they could at least be friends, but innate honesty forced her to admit that she wanted much more from him. She had only known him for a few hours but he had tilted her world. She had no experience of love, but this intense physical desire for Jake, this flood of feeling that consumed all her senses, had to be love or something very like it.

In her work with International Rapid Rescue she had witnessed death and destruction on a huge scale. If the job had taught her anything, it was that life was precious but could be snuffed out in an instant by an act of nature. She was a twenty-six-year-old virgin, probably because all her life she had been a tomboy and the few men she knew considered her more of a buddy than a woman. She was not totally inexperienced—she had kissed men, but had thought the experience vastly overrated. But all that had changed last night when she had met Jake.

This holiday, the first she had taken in years, was supposed to be a complete change, a chance to rethink her hectic lifestyle. She was her own woman; she could do whatever she wanted, and what she wanted was Jake. She knew deep down on some elemental level that Jake could be her soul mate.

The voice of the doorman boomed over the intercom telling her a Mr d'Amato had arrived and should he send him up? She dashed to answer it. 'No need, I'll be right down.'

Her legs were shaking as she rode the lift to the ground floor and when the doors opened Charlie drew in a deep, calming breath, stepped out, and froze to the spot, her blue eyes fixed on the spectacular male animal leaning against the reception desk.

In a business suit Jake had looked stunning, but today he took her breath away. He was wearing black jeans that lovingly clung to long legs and taut, masculine thighs. A black button-down shirt, left open at the neck, revealed the strong column of his throat, and a black leather jacket fitting casually across broad shoulders completed the picture.

Telling her foolish heart to stop bounding, she wondered what it was about Italian men that enabled them to wear clothes with such casual elegance. She could not tear her fascinated gaze away. She saw his proud head lift as though scenting the air like some great jungle beast suddenly aware of his prey, and, straightening up, he turned towards her.

'Charlotta-a…at last.' He lingered over her name like a caress, his hooded dark eyes sweeping over her in blatant masculine appraisal as in a few lithe strides he covered the space between them. 'You look exquisite.' Before she could draw breath, a large male hand curved around her hips, another up her back to tangle in the loose fall of her hair.

The swift, exquisitely gentle brush of Jake's lips against her own turned her legs to jelly, and when he teased her lips apart, the arousing sweep of his tongue in the moist interior of her mouth suddenly filled her body with a molten heat.

Charlie had thought the kisses they had shared in the car last night mind-blowing. But now, held in intimate contact with every hard inch of his big powerful frame, she was shocked by the force of his obvious arousal and secretly thrilled she could do that to him. Weak at the knees with wanting, she pressed unconsciously closer into his taut strength, and felt his great chest heave.

'I promised you lunch,' Jake rasped against her mouth and lifted his head.

Charlie stared up. 'What?' she murmured, flicking the tip of her tongue along her bottom lip, an invitation in her sapphire gaze she didn't realise was there.

'Lunch.' Jake stepped back, his hands resting on her shoulders to keep her steady. 'Before we really give the doorman something to talk about.'

Realising where she was and that she was staring at him far too hungrily, she dipped her head, a tide of red scorching her cheeks. 'Yes, of course,' she mumbled.

'A lady who can still blush. I like it,' Jake drawled, keeping an arm around her shoulder as he walked her out of the building.

'No car?' Charlie queried as his arm fell from her shoulders and he took her hand in his and began strolling along the pavement.

Jake looked at her, amused indulgence in his gaze. 'Your wish is my command,' he said smoothly. 'You wanted to do the tourist bit, and visit the museum. Most tourists pound the pavement. No?' He shrugged his elegant shoulders. 'Plus I want to share everything with you, starting with a bottle of wine with lunch.'

He looked so attractive, and so unlike any tourist she had ever seen, Charlie burst out laughing. 'I might have known you would have an ulterior motive. It's not me but the wine that motivates you.'

'You wouldn't believe my motives if I told you,' Jake responded dryly and spun her into his arms to kiss her with an urgency that left her dazed and breathless—so dazed she did not see the cynicism in his dark eyes. And for Charlie the kiss set the pattern for the rest of the day.

Jake kept his word and they shared a bottle of wine over lunch at the restaurant in the central courtyard of the British Museum. After lingering over coffee and cognac they eventually got around to touring the various exhibits.

It was seven in the evening when they walked back to his hotel.

The warmth of his arm felt so right around her waist, and when he stopped and asked, 'What's it to be, Charlotte? Dinner with me here or do you want to walk on to your apartment?' they both knew what he was really asking. The whole day had been leading to this point.

Charlie raised her face to him and saw her own need reflected in the gleaming depths of his dark eyes. The force of emotion flooding through her kept her speechless for a moment.

'We can call it a day,' Jake heard himself say in a sudden surprising attack of conscience. Amazingly, he had enjoyed Charlotte's company. In different circumstances he knew he would have dated her anyway—and he would still have been determined to get her into his bed.

He reached out and ran a long finger over her smooth cheek, and down her throat, his finger resting on the rapidly pounding pulse in her neck. She wanted him, he knew it, but she was still hesitating. Real or acting he did not know, but he knew enough about women to realise they all craved permanency in a relationship. Obviously Charlotte was no different. She was here on holiday and seemed determined to follow the tourist trail—and his quick brain had the answer.

He smiled, an intimate curl of his firm lips. 'Whatever you decide. I am staying in London for a couple of weeks on business.' He slowly raked her body with his gaze, registering the burgeoning peaks of her breasts beneath her sweater before he let his eyes meet hers. 'And after the great time we have had today…' He paused, his hand softly caressing her throat. 'Work permitting, I would love to explore the tourist trail with you, Charlotte.'

The only trail he was really interested in exploring was every curve of her delectable body, every hill and hidden valley, until he sated himself in her. But he wasn't crazy enough to tell her so. Though if he did not have her soon, he very well might, and that *really* worried him.

In the early hours of the morning Charlie had decided to pursue her relationship with Jake and see where it led, and all day she had fallen deeper and deeper under his spell. Now, with the impact of Jake's deep eyes burning down into hers, and his huskily voiced desire to see her again echoing in her head, she knew it was the moment of truth. He had told her last night he would never marry, so either she had to accept what he was offering, an affair for a couple of weeks, or walk away. With blinding clarity she realised she did not have a choice. She could no longer deny her basic sexual instinct, an instinct she had only just discovered she possessed, an instinct she knew deep down inside she would only ever feel with Jake.

Charlie drew in a slow steadying breath. 'I've done enough walking for one day.'

'Me too.' Reaching for her hand once more, he linked his long fingers through hers and led her into the hotel.

On one level Charlie couldn't believe what she was doing as Jake ushered her into the lift and the metal doors closed on them. But on another purely sensual level the feelings were so immense she could not deny them, however much she tried. She stole a surreptitious glance at him through the thick veil of her lashes. He was so ruggedly attractive, so overtly masculine, simply looking at him made her heart beat faster. It wasn't just his looks, though; she had seen men with more classically beautiful features. It was some unfathomable intense connection she could hardly believe was real. But every atom in her body was telling her it was.

'This is it,' Jake said, dropping her hand and splaying his palm across the small of her back, his powerful body tense as he urged her out of the lift to a door directly opposite. A quick flash of the card key and she was in his suite. He fought the instinct to simply sweep her off her feet and into the bedroom. Instead he shrugged off his jacket as he headed for the bar.

'What would you like to drink?' he asked, turning back to look at her, and stiffened. Damn it, but she was gorgeous, and the way she filled that pink sweater had been causing him agony all day.

Standing where he had left her Charlie glanced around the elegant room. It was as luxurious as she had expected. But Jake's behaviour was not what she had imagined. She had thought he would sweep her into his arms, and make mad, passionate love to her. How naive was that? she castigated herself. Jake was a sophisticated man of the world, a man of discernment; of course he would never behave so crassly, she thought. But she was wrong again.

'I'll—' She was going to ask for a glass of juice, but she never got the chance.

'To hell with a drink,' he growled and in a couple of lithe strides he reached her and hauled her hard against his chest. His expert mouth swooped down to capture hers, a soft moan escaped her, and, taking full advantage, his tongue slipped between her parted lips with devastating effect.

Charlie did not know what hit her. Before his kisses had excited her, but had ended abruptly and left her aching for more. This time Jake showed no such restraint. His tongue swirled around hers, igniting a passion that was red hot. His arms were tight around her, pressing her against his aroused body, telling her without words how much he wanted her. Her slender hands lifted to his broad chest, a finger catching on his shirt button.

She felt his smile as he murmured against her lips, 'Go ahead, take it off for me.' His dark eyes gleamed down into hers, an invitation explicit in the black depths.

Feverish colour flooded Charlie's face, and she was stunned to realise he actually thought she was experienced enough to undress him without a qualm. Her body burned and her finger flexed against his chest. Dared she? Yes—this was what she wanted. She freed one button, and her stomach somersaulted as her fingers scraped the hot skin beneath.

'Don't stop now, *cara*,' Jake husked, his hands sliding caressingly up and down her back. 'Or perhaps you prefer I undress you first?' His sensuous mouth swooped down to taste hers again, and went lower to nuzzle the elegant curve of her neck, and Charlie stifled a frustrated groan when he broke the connection.

'Patience, *cara*,' he teased, a knowing smile curving his firm mouth. 'First let me get rid of this damn belt.' One strong hand slid around her waist. 'It could do a man a serious injury,' he added, his fingers deftly unfastening the buckle, and the offending item fell to the floor. 'Now tell me what you want, and I promise I will oblige.'

What she wanted was Jake, and her fingers, with a dexterity she did not know she possessed, swiftly unbuttoned his shirt. Then she stopped, her blue eyes widening to their fullest extent at the sight of a wedge of broad tanned chest, and the dusting of soft black curls that accentuated his powerful pectoral muscles. She swayed against him, her hands tentatively splaying on his naked chest. She could feel the heat through her palms, and her awed gaze lifted to his. 'You are beautiful,' she murmured softly.

'I think that is my line,' Jake mocked, but his eyes glinted with a hint of masculine satisfaction and something more. His dark head bent and his lips brushed across hers as he gathered her hard against him, and kissed her long and deep. So deep that when he suddenly eased her away from the heat of his great body, she was breathless, her legs felt like rubber and she could hardly stand.

But she didn't need to.

CHAPTER FOUR

'THIS is not the place,' Jake said and swept Charlie up in his arms. 'And we have too many clothes on,' he added with a teasing grin as he strode into the bedroom and lowered her down against him onto her own feet, before stepping back, kicking off his shoes and shrugging out of his shirt.

The partial view of his broad chest had not prepared her for the awesome beauty of his naked torso. Mesmerised, she simply stared. His shoulders were wide, his chest broad and tapering down to a lean waist, his skin gleaming like burnished gold in stark contrast to the mass of black curling hair arrowing down his strong body. His long arms were hard and muscular and had their own dusting of hair. His hands…his hands were unfastening his trousers. Charlie gasped, her heart skipping a beat.

'Something wrong, *mia bella Charlotta*?' His hands settled on her waist and Charlie was glad of the support, shaken by the intensity of her own desire for him.

'No,' she murmured. 'Never more right.' She strove to match his sophistication but her voice shook ever so slightly.

'But you still have too many clothes on, *cara*.' A slow, sensuous smile curved his wide mouth, his eyes gleaming beneath black curling lashes. 'Let me help you,' he suggested throatily as his fingers caught the edge of her sweater and he eased it up from her hips.

Hypnotised by the intensity of his dark gaze, like a puppet on a string, Charlie raised her arms and he slipped the sweater over her head. His hands stroked down her naked back, and her bra went the same way as the sweater.

'Magnificent,' Jake husked as his hands swept round and up to cup her high, firm breasts.

Charlie sucked in a feverish breath, her breasts suddenly heavy, the small nipples swelling and tightening into pinpoints of pleasure. She had never imagined she could stand brazenly half naked before a man and, lifting her eyes, she felt her cheeks flood with colour at his intent masculine scrutiny.

'You have nothing to blush about, *cara*.' His smouldering gaze met hers, his voice fracturing a little. 'You have perfect breasts, and I can't wait to see the rest of you.'

'Nor me you,' she mumbled inanely, and she got her wish.

Jake lowered his hands from her breasts, but not before rubbing her tight, swollen nipples with skilful fingers as he kissed her again with erotic thoroughness before pulling back from her and calmly stripping off.

Faced by a totally naked Jake, she could not stop staring. He was all hard muscle, and sleek golden skin, from his broad chest down to his taut, flat stomach, and lean hips. A ribbon of paler skin circled the top of his powerful thighs. So he didn't sunbathe nude, she thought, and it was her last sensible thought.

Eyes widening, her face burning along with every other inch of her body, for the first time in her life she was confronted by a magnificently virile aroused male and she could not tear her gaze away.

'You're lagging behind,' Jake said with a husky chuckle. As she hastily lifted her head her entranced blue eyes connected with sensuous black and she couldn't say a word. 'Here, let me help you,' he added and skimmed her trousers and briefs down her hips with a deftness that spelt of years of practice. He gathered her up in his arms and laid her on the bed.

'Unbelievable,' Jake murmured, staring down at the silky softness of her creamy skin, and the rosy-tipped peaks of her lush breasts. For a second embarrassment overcame Charlie and she lifted her hands to cover herself from his scorching gaze.

'No, don't,' Jake growled. Sitting down beside her, he took her hands and pressed them onto the bed, one each side of her head. His dark gaze swept her. Her body was curvaceous yet toned to perfection with firm, beautifully shaped breasts, a narrow waist, flaring hips and fabulous long legs. 'You are absolutely stunning,' he said throatily, his gaze roaming back up over her incredible body and lingering on tight rosy nipples before lifting to her face. 'And so very sexy.' And he covered her mouth with his own.

The feel of his long hard body against hers, and the magic of his firm, sensuous mouth, his tongue tangling with hers, the taste of him… Charlie lost her every last inhibition. She tried to pull her hands free. 'Please, I want to touch you,' she said with a naive honesty.

'Feel free.' Jake grinned and let go of her hands, his heavy-lidded eyes gleaming into hers. 'I certainly intend to touch every part of you, my sweet Charlotte, in every way.' Dipping his head, he trailed kisses down her throat, sucking on the tiny pulse racing beneath her silken skin, before moving lower and licking and nipping the rosy nipples with his teeth and tongue, while his hand stroked down the curve of her waist and traced her inner thigh.

Charlie buried her hands in the thick dark hair of his head, her spine arching up to him, and she groaned out loud at the exquisite sensations lancing from her breast to the apex of her thighs. He kissed and caressed a sensuous path from her breasts to her navel, and traced the line of her hip and thigh right down to the soles of her feet with a hungry, erotic thoroughness that made her wriggle and squirm in feverish delight, before returning to her mouth and kissing her with a driving, possessive passion that she met and matched with helpless abandon.

She wrapped her arms tight around him, on fire for him. Her hands swept over the wide muscular shoulders, traced the indentation of his spine, and splayed over the strong shoulder blades. She pressed up into him and, with an eroticism she had never dreamt she was capable of, rubbed her achingly sensitised breasts against the hard wall of his chest, glorying in the excitement the friction aroused.

It was as if some other female had taken over, a sexy, liberated female, and she nuzzled into the hard curve of his shoulder, and moaned as his fingers toyed with her breast once more. When the hand on her thigh slipped ever closer to the centre of her femininity, she shivered in delicious anticipation. She was damp and hot and aching for him and her legs moved apart instinctively. Her head burrowed lower, looking for a taut male nipple, one hand sliding over his lean hips searching for something else.

Jake's hand tangled in her hair and urged her head up. 'Not so fast, *cara*.' He laughed softly, his face inches from hers. 'I want to make this good for you, to make it last.'

With passion-dazed eyes she looked into his face, the smouldering black eyes, the dishevelled hair that she was responsible for, and the wickedly sinful mouth smiling down. It was the smile that goaded her even as her insides were melting like hot treacle. Daringly her slender fingers inched around his hip and touched the long velvet shaft, and she heard him groan. 'Why wait?' she prompted breathlessly, her sapphire eyes widening to blaze with a need and knowledge as old as Eve. 'We can always do it again.'

Jake was not made of stone, though at that moment he was as hard as any rock. He caught her hand and lifted it up to his chest, though it nearly killed him to do so. *Dio*, but she was a temptress, and she was right. Once would never be enough with this woman, he knew, and he took her teasing mouth with a savage hunger he could barely control.

Charlie fought to drag air into her starving lungs as he broke the kiss, his head swooping down, his tongue flicking over her aching breasts once more, even as his long fingers eased through the golden curls at the junction of her thighs, and expertly stroked the moist feminine heart of her. She wrapped her arms around him and clung, her hips rising from the bed, as with torturous strokes he teased and probed her tight, silken depths until she was sure she could stand no more. Her body was white hot and wound up so tight she felt she would shatter into a million pieces with sensual excitement.

Jake lifted his head, his eyes molten pools of black jet, his bronzed skin flushed along his high cheekbones. 'You want me.'

'I'm crazy for you,' she groaned. He rose over her, and she was unaware he reached for something from the bedside table as the subtle stroke of his lean fingers took her to the edge again.

'Yes,' Jake rasped and in one smooth motion he grasped her hips, and lifted her.

She felt the hard length of him touch her, stroke her once, twice. Her whole body shuddered, and she drew in an audible breath as with one powerful move he entered her.

Jake stilled as a gasp of protest escaped her. He was a big man to accommodate, he knew, and she was so tight that the thought crossed his mind it must have been some time since she had indulged. He pulled back ever so slightly, and eased into her slow and deep, and felt her silken muscles clench around him.

The sudden slight pain had caught Charlie by surprise, but was instantly forgotten as Jake stroked deeper, and in that moment she lost it completely. She cried out loud, 'Oh, yes, Jake, yes,' at the incredible sensations convulsing her slender body with a fierce pleasure that shattered all her innocent illusions, and left her shuddering in ecstasy. So this was…it. But the thought never fully formed, as Jake plunged harder and faster in a wild, primitive rhythm that drove her higher and higher.

Charlie clung to him in a fever of need, oblivious to the fact her nails were digging into his flesh. She felt as if he were lifting her out of herself to a realm where nothing existed but his hot, hard body filling her, possessing her. And she was totally unaware of the breathless plea for more escaping her as he captured the erotic sound with his mouth. She felt his great body shudder violently, and she cried out his name as wave after wave of explosive sensations swept her into an ecstatic oblivion.

Slowly Charlie opened her eyes. Jake was collapsed on top of her, his eyes closed. But even so she smiled mistily up at him. So that was it, the little death she had read about, and it was all, and much, much more than she could have ever imagined.

Their bodies were damp with perspiration, their hearts thundering in the aftermath of passion, and a deep sense of peace washed over her. Jake was the man she was born for, she thought dreamily.

'*Grazie*, Charlotte,' Jake murmured close to her ear, burying his face in the silken, fragrant mass of her hair for a moment. 'That was fantastic.' He smoothed the tumbled hair from her brow. 'I was right, you are some woman.' He eased his heavy body from hers, and from the bed.

'Don't go,' Charlie murmured, reaching out a hand to him.

'Don't worry, I am not going far.' Jake stood, unashamedly naked, looking down at her. 'I am only going to the bathroom to dispense with this and replenish supplies. Unless you would like to do it for me,' he suggested teasingly.

Sprawled on the bed totally naked, she looked dazedly up into his grinning face, registering the black hair flopping over his brow, the smouldering eyes, and the wickedly masculine mouth. He was utterly gorgeous and he was hers. Her eyes roamed leisurely down the naked length of him and only then did the import of his words sink in.

'No, I don't think so,' she squeaked. Of course he had used protection—it was nothing to be embarrassed about, in fact she should be grateful, but it did not stop her blushing scarlet and dragging the sheet up over her naked body.

Jake let out a bark of laughter. 'You're incredible—sex on legs and verbal with it, and yet you blush like a schoolgirl.' He shook his dark head. 'That is some trick.' And he headed for the bathroom.

Charlie didn't know whether to be flattered because he thought she was incredible and sexy, or affronted because he thought her blushing was a trick. If only, she thought ruefully. Blushing was the bane of her life. Perhaps now she was truly a woman the blushing would cease, and that led her to another thought. How come Jake hadn't realised he was her first lover? Not that it mattered; she was quite flattered that he seemed to think she was experienced. She had a sneaking suspicion that if he had known the truth he would not have touched her, and it crossed her mind to wonder how old he was. Mid thirties, she guessed, with a great body. A body she now knew in every intimate detail. A reminiscent smile curved her soft mouth that quickly changed into a triumphant grin. At last she was truly a woman—Jake's woman, she thought, a sense of euphoria sweeping through her. The sheet forgotten, she punched her arms up in the air. 'Yes, yes, yes!'

Jake strode back into the bedroom, a towelling robe tied loosely around his waist, and stopped. With her blonde hair cascading down her back, natural he now knew, and her beautiful face devoid of make-up, she was punching the air like some crazed cheerleader when her team scored a goal.

She was the most naturally sexy woman he had ever known, and he was a long way from finished with her yet. But she looked about sixteen, and he found himself grinning. 'Is that yes for me?' he asked with a chuckle, which quickly turned into a shout of laughter as her startled blue eyes swung towards him, and she dived back beneath the covers.

'No. Yes. I mean, maybe,' Charlie babbled, appalled he had caught her acting like an idiot instead of the sophisticated lady she wanted to appear.

'Well, make your mind up, *cara*,' Jake prompted. 'I'm hungry.' It wasn't food he had in mind. With her beautiful hair spread across the pillow, and her face scarlet with embarrassment, he had the oddest urge to protect her—

and, as the instant stirring in his groin reminded him, every which way.

The thought disturbed him and his heavy brows drew together in a frown. His initial intention had been simply to get Charlotte into bed and then dismiss her. But it hadn't worked out quite like that. With her exquisite body shuddering beneath him, her silken sheath so hot, so tight, the restraint he had imposed upon himself had deserted him completely. A captive to his own desire, he had taken her with a driven power he was helpless to control, and when she had convulsed around him, sobbing his name, he had gone with her, something that rarely happened to him.

Even now he was itching to slip back into bed beside her and start all over again. No wonder Anna had been so besotted with Robert Summerville. If the man had been anything like the natural-born sensualist his daughter was, it was not surprising Anna had become addicted to the man.

Remembering Anna and the way Charlotte had hurt her by refusing to meet her stopped Jake in his tracks. The Charlotte he had spent the day with and just made love to didn't seem to be a selfish bitch, but then experience had taught him women were great deceivers.

'I'll go and order dinner. Join me when you're ready,' Jake said bluntly, and, spinning on his heel, he left the room.

Charlie stared at his back, shocked by his abrupt departure. She had behaved like an overgrown schoolgirl. No wonder Jake had opted for food. Still, the night was young, she thought, a secret smile curving her swollen lips, and Jake was her lover. She stretched in preparation of rising from the bed. A shower, food, and Jake again…sounded good. Rolling out of bed, she collected her clothes and headed for the bathroom.

It was a splendid bathroom, all veined white marble and mirrors, with a huge glass-fronted shower stall. Reaching into the stall, she turned on the taps. With the water running at a comfortable temperature, she rifled among the luxurious toiletries provided and found aromatherapy soap. A touch of pampering was just what she needed, Charlie told herself, and stepped under the soothing spray, a deep sigh of satisfaction escaping her.

So this was love. She sighed, let her head fall back and closed her eyes, and began slowly lathering her arms, shoulders, and her firm breasts. She stroked the tender skin, and revived the memory of Jake touching her there—everywhere—and the incredible power of his passion, and she almost groaned.

Jake tipped the bellboy, and strode back into the bedroom. The bed was empty, and inexplicably his stomach knotted painfully, and his eyes darkened angrily. She was gone. Then he heard the sound of running water, and common sense prevailed. Of course she was in the shower.

For a moment there he hadn't been thinking straight, but now he was. Silently he entered the *en suite*, and for a moment was disorientated, his body tensing at the sight of Charlotte's silhouette reflected several times over in the mirrored walls. Then he saw her behind the glass screen. Her head was thrown back, her hair falling wet and sleek down her back, and her hands were running over her breasts, her body. He had never seen anything more erotic in his life, but it was the look of sensual pleasure on her beautiful face that aroused him with gut-wrenching speed.

Charlie didn't hear the bathroom door open. The first intimation she had she was not alone was when a husky voice declared from behind her, 'Allow me.'

Her eyes flew open and she spun around, her feet slipping on the tiled floor, and only Jake's arm around her waist saved her from falling. 'What are you doing?' she exclaimed. He was naked, the water flattening his black hair into a sleek cap, and his dark eyes burnt with sensual promise.

'Just what you were doing, my sweet Charlotte.' Somehow he had the soap in his hand and was rubbing it against her breasts. 'Washing you.' He dropped the soap and his hand began to lather the soft bubbles over her swelling breasts. 'Now, isn't that better?' Jake growled.

'Oh, yes,' Charlie sighed. Her body was hot, and it had nothing to do with the water, and everything to do with a naked Jake pressing her back against the cubicle wall, his hands administering a leisurely soaping to her quivering body. Her breasts felt heavy and swollen, and the straining peaks tautened into hard points of aching need. 'Don't stop.'

With a throaty laugh Jake bent his head, and took her softly parted lips with a leashed hunger that quickly deepened into a hard, possessive kiss. 'I am not going to,' he rasped, and, with all pretence of washing gone, he lifted her bodily and placed her legs around his lean waist.

'No, I'll fall,' she squealed, and grabbed for his head, linking her arms around his neck. But she didn't fall as his strong hands cupped her hips and in one smooth thrust he filled her. Her eyes closed and her head fell back as her legs locked around him, his swift possession engulfing her quivering body in a wave of crazy excitement.

Jake growled low in his throat. Passion riding him, he drove hard and fast, and cried out her name as he climaxed with embarrassing speed. Her body shuddered in convulsive ecstasy around him, draining him to the core.

Gently he steadied her on her feet, his hands almost spanning her slender waist. She was looking up at him, her gorgeous blue eyes dilated with shock. 'I shouldn't have done that,' he murmured.

'In the shower,' Charlie breathed incredulously. 'I didn't know you could,' she added, dazed but happy.

'Apparently around you, anywhere will do,' Jake remarked, realising she was nowhere near as experienced as he had thought if she had never shared a shower with a man. Suddenly he wondered just how much she had shared with other men as he recalled her pained gasp the first time they had sex. The uneasy feeling he might have just made a huge mistake made his hands tighten involuntarily around her waist, and he surveyed her with a frown. Her incredible blue eyes were sparkling cheekily up at him, and she had the sexiest body he had ever seen. No, it wasn't possible. He shook his dark head, dismissing the notion. 'Actually, I came to tell you dinner had arrived, but I got distracted.'

'You and me both,' Charlie quipped, and reached up to press a kiss on his jaw. 'But now get out and let me get dried and dressed.' The fact that Jake could be overcome with passion for her made her proud, and fed her confidence in herself as a woman.

But her confidence took a severe nosedive ten minutes later when she padded barefoot back into the sitting room of the suite. Jake was fully dressed in a white shirt and dark blue pleated trousers, and somehow she felt at a disadvantage wearing the same sweater and trousers she had worn all day. He was seated on one of the two sofas with the dinner trolley set between them and he did not acknowledge her at all. It was only when she sat down on the sofa opposite him that he deigned to glance at her.

'This is probably not so hot now,' he said, but he might have been talking to a stranger. 'If you don't mind waiting, I can order something else before you leave.'

Leave. Her heart sank. But she told herself not to be so foolish. Think of the embarrassment if she did stay all night and had to walk through the hotel in the morning. Everyone would know what she had been doing. No, Jake was simply being a gentleman. But then she saw his dark eyes, which held no warmth or tenderness, none of the passion they had recently shared, only a cool reserve.

She shivered. 'This will do fine.' She gestured to the trolley, and wondered why she should suddenly feel such a chill. 'I'm not very hungry.'

'Good, but you must eat something.' He lifted the covers and portioned some kind of meat casserole and vegetables onto a plate and handed it to her. His mouth smiled but his eyes did not. 'Enjoy.'

Feeling worse by the minute, Charlie took the plate and stared down at it, sure it would choke her. But she forced herself to eat, her mind searching for a reason for his cool behaviour. Perhaps he was just naturally subdued after making love, she tried to tell herself, but without much conviction as she recalled how several times over dinner last night he had behaved in much the same way, a certain remoteness in his dark gaze effectively masking his expression.

'You're very quiet,' she offered.

'I'm eating,' Jake said with a sardonic arch of an ebony brow in her direction, and she watched as he dug into the casserole with apparent enjoyment.

Turning back to her own plate, she swallowed a few more mouthfuls. But it tasted like sawdust in her mouth, and she placed it back on the trolley. It must be her fault Jake was so reserved, but what had she done wrong? Perhaps Jake had seen through her attempt to be sophisticated and was disappointed at her performance in bed. She had read men put great store on a woman's abilities in bed, and Jake was no boy; he must have slept with a lot of women.

'How old are you?' she blurted, and bit her lip wishing she could take the question back. But at least it got his full attention.

'Thirty-eight. Probably old enough to be your father.' His voice held a sharp edge of contempt that she could not fail to recognise.

Suddenly everything became clear and her heart lifted. Jake, her sophisticated, powerful Jake, was feeling guilty about the age difference between them. Impulsively she jumped to her feet and sat on the sofa beside him, resting her hand on his thigh, determined to reassure him. 'Not unless you started before you were a teenager,' she said, glancing up at his superb profile. 'I'm twenty-six, hardly a girl.'

Jake turned his head and looked down at the small hand on his thigh and then up into her smiling face. 'You think there is nothing wrong in an older man taking a much younger woman for a lover?' he asked with such bitterness in his voice that she was shocked.

'Not if he…' She was going to say *loves her*, but stopped. 'Not if he really wants her and the feeling is mutual. No,' she said carefully, not confident enough to imply Jake loved her. But she did want to convince him his age didn't matter.

'You honestly believe that.'

'Yes, of course,' she said firmly.

'Probably only because you had to put up with a father who had quite a few young lovers. Does it never occur to you other people may not share your views?' he queried with a cynical drawl.

'No, not really. And as for my father, he was a law unto himself, and I never had to put up with his lovers. I only ever met one,' Charlie said honestly. 'But we're not talking about him, but you.' She found it incredible to believe a man as stunning as Jake should feel vulnerable about his age and yet it endeared him to her all the more.

'Are we?' Jake said with a sardonic arch of an eyebrow. Charlotte had just confirmed what Anna had told him. *She never had to put up with her father's lovers.* She was the selfish bitch after all. But as he looked down into her earnest sapphire eyes, and with her hand on his thigh, somehow confronting her with what he knew didn't seem important. Instead he imagined her slender hand gliding up his thigh. Fighting down the sudden jerk of excitement in his groin, he backtracked swiftly. 'If you say so.'

The veiled statement confused her. 'Well, why else would you mention the age difference?'

Jake flung her a dazzling smile and put his arm around her shoulders. 'No reason at all, Charlotte, *cara*. You're right, what is twelve years between friends?' But, looking into his dark eyes, she had the uneasy feeling he was not telling the truth, but simply placating her. Then he tilted her chin with one finger and brushed his lips lightly against hers.

Charlie exhaled a relieved sigh at the touch of his mouth and eagerly parted her lips and Jake took full advantage, probing the moist depths with a leisurely expertise that squashed all her irrational doubts about him.

'If I don't get you out of here soon,' Jake groaned against her ear, 'I'll take you on the sofa.'

CHAPTER FIVE

THE image Jake conjured up in Charlie's head was explicitly erotic, and sent her pulse rate rocketing. Heat curled in her belly and her slender fingers involuntarily flexed and stroked up his muscular thigh.

Dark eyes flaring, Jake drew in a harsh breath and leapt to his feet, his square jaw set at a determined angle. 'It is time I sent you home.'

Blinded by lust, he had already taken her in the shower without thought of the consequences, and, looking into her sultry blue eyes, he had very nearly slid into her hot little body yet again. A warning voice in his head told him he had to regain control of his suddenly overactive libido around Charlotte or he was in danger of making another mistake. 'I'll call you a cab,' he said curtly, and surprised himself by trying to soften the abrupt dismissal with the lame excuse, 'I have to work tomorrow.'

Charlie slumped back against the sofa and looked up at him with wide, puzzled eyes. A moment ago he had been looking at her as if he could eat her alive, but now his eyes were shuttered, and she could sense the disapproval in the firm set of his jaw. What was it he had said, something about working? 'But tomorrow is Sunday,' she murmured inanely.

A black brow elevated. 'So?'

The heat in her stomach turned into a cold knot of humiliation as it slowly dawned on her she had overstayed her welcome and he was trying to give her a polite brush-off. Rising to her feet, she avoided looking at him. 'I'll just be a minute. I need my shoes and bag from the bedroom, then I'll leave you in peace.'

As she attempted to walk past him Jake closed a strong brown hand around her wrist and prevented her from moving away. He saw the hurt she could not hide in her expressive eyes and he knew exactly what she was thinking.

'Peace is not something I will ever associate with you, *cara*,' he said with a rueful shake of his dark head. Wanting her was a weakness. He had every reason to dislike her, but she turned him on like no other woman he had ever known, and he'd wanted her from the minute he had set eyes on her. He still wanted her and only a fool turned down what she was offering.

He was no fool, though he had been acting like one for the past half-hour, torn between conscience and chemistry. Chemistry won as Jake curved her own wrist around her back and drew her close to him again. 'Your effect on me is quite the opposite, and I like the way you make me feel.'

'You really do?' Charlie queried uncertainly, a tide of red sweeping up over her pale face as her body responded with quivering eagerness to the powerful strength of his embrace. She was hopelessly confused. She couldn't understand why he blew hot and cold. She couldn't understand men, full stop! she thought helplessly.

With a husky chuckle Jake bent his dark head. 'If you need me to confirm it after the past few hours, then I obviously have not fulfilled your expectations.' And he took her shocked open mouth with his in a display of erotic expertise that left her in no doubt of his desire for her.

'This is madness,' Jake groaned a moment later, lifting his head to look down at her with stormy black eyes. 'But you are a fire in my blood and I can't resist you.'

Charlie should have been flattered by his comment, but there was something suspiciously like resentment in his dark gaze that sounded warning bells in her head. He was a gorgeous virile male, streets ahead of her in experience and sophistication, and yet he said it was madness. Perhaps it was! She had fallen headlong in love with him, but what did she really know about him? Other than that he was a fabulous lover and they had come together with what some, herself included, would say was unseemly haste, since meeting two days ago!

'Maybe I should leave,' she said stiffly. 'It's late.'

After he had admitted he was burning for her, not a confession he usually made, Jake was disconcerted by her sudden about-face. Dark colour flared over his high cheekbones, and he drew in a ragged breath and relaxed his hold on her. Having spent years calling the shots with the women in his life, he found it a salutary experience to have Charlotte do the same to him. His heavy-lidded eyes half closed as he stepped back and glanced at his wrist-watch. 'You're right, it's after one—there's no point waiting for a cab. I'll drive you home.'

Charlie thought she had offended him, so the relief she felt was immense when he drew up outside the apartment block with a squeal of brakes and turned to her. 'Thank you for a wonderful day, Charlotte, and an even better evening. Give me your number and I will call you tomorrow. Something so good should not be ignored.' He grinned.

Quickly she withdrew a business card and pen from her purse, and wrote Dave's number on the back. She also took out her door key.

'Home and here,' she murmured as Jake took the card from her fingers, and slid out of the car to walk around the bonnet and open the passenger door.

'Come on, Charlotte.' He held out his hand and, relieved, she took it and walked up the steps to the entrance foyer.

She swiped the card through the slot, and the glass doors slid open. 'Good evening, Miss Summerville,' the security guard on the reception desk called out. Charlie returned the greeting, and then glanced back at Jake, reluctant to part from him but not sure how to proceed. Stupid, she knew, when not long ago she had been in bed with the man, but she couldn't help it. Before Jake she had imagined love to be some perfect life-enhancing dream; the insecurity she now felt had not been part of it.

Sensing her dilemma, Jake cupped her face in his hands, and brushed his lips to hers. 'Goodnight.' He felt her tremble and smiled. 'I'll call.' And he left.

His smile and gentle kiss lingered on her lips like a benediction and when she reached her apartment she fell into bed and slept like the proverbial log.

Charlie yawned and stretched, then groaned. She ached in places she never knew she had. *Jake.* She murmured his name, and images of the previous day ran like a video recording through her mind. A deep, shuddering sigh escaped her and even the fine cotton cover felt too warm on her overheated flesh.

She glanced at the bedside clock, and looked again. Ten o'clock! She had overslept big time. Jake might have already called, and, leaping off the bed, she dashed into the shower. She dressed with feverish haste in her favourite blue jeans and a white cotton shirt, and swept her hair up in a pony-tail. She looked at herself in the mirror as she rubbed a light moisturiser into her face and paused, noting the sparkle in her eyes, the flush of excitement along her delicate cheekbones, and marvelled at the difference having a man in her life had made. Her total transformation from a brisk, efficient young woman to the hungry, sensuous creature that smiled back at her took some getting used to. Still smiling, she walked into the tiny kitchen and pressed the call retrieve button on the wall-mounted telephone. Her smile faded as the automated voice informed her, 'No messages.'

She switched on the coffee percolator and consoled herself with the fact Jake had said he was going to work. Then she discovered she had no milk. She disliked black coffee, but she managed to drink one cup, and ate an apple, the only food in the place. She really should do some shopping, but she was too afraid to leave the apartment in case she missed Jake's call.

She washed her cup before strolling back into the living area. It took her all of ten minutes to tidy it up, then, ascending the stairs to the galleried sleeping area, she made the bed. For the next two hours she paced the apartment, one minute elated, sure he would call, and the next moment in despair, convinced he wouldn't.

Finally by midday she realised she was behaving like a besotted idiot. She needed milk, and, grabbing her bag and keys, she took the lift to the ground floor. The doorman told her where the nearest convenience store was and she stepped out into the spring sunshine, telling herself if Jake did call he would probably leave his number and she could call him back, no problem.

The store was a lot further than the doorman had made it sound, and it was an hour later when Charlie, a carrier bag in one hand, her head bent in gloom, trudged back into her apartment building.

'Buon giorno, cara.' The deep, melodious voice was music to her ears, and her head shot up. 'I see the wanderer has returned.'

Jake was waiting in the foyer. He strolled towards her and stared down at her from his great height, a slow smile curving across his handsome face. 'Charlotte.'

As he said her name Charlie's heart beat a frenzied tattoo in her chest and she blushed, as the memory of last night seemed all too real. He was here, inches away from her; she could reach out and touch him.

'Let me help you with that.' He took the carrier from her hand, and smiled wryly when he saw the expression on her face. His dark head bent and he brushed his lips lightly against her cheek. 'I called to see if you would like to have lunch with me.' His deep accented drawl and the promise in the dark eyes that met hers made her ache for so much more.

'Jake. You're here.' She finally found her voice. 'I thought you were going to ring.'

He straightened up, and the eyes that held hers were suddenly dark and unfathomable. 'I hope I have not called at an inconvenient moment, interrupted anything.'

'No, not at all,' she hastened to reassure him, her eyes sliding lovingly over him, taking in the casual cream trousers and the open-necked, slightly darker polo shirt that revealed the perfect musculature of his chest. She swallowed hard and said, 'Come on up. I only have to put the milk in the fridge and then I'm yours.'

'You're sure about that?' Jake demanded. 'If you're involved with someone else, say so now, Charlotte.'

She shook her head. 'Of course not.' She could sense the sudden tension in him, and wondered at its cause. 'Whatever gave you that idea?'

'Maybe because you are staying in another man's apartment.'

She laughed in relief. 'Oh, Dave is just a very old friend.'

'Then I trust he stays that way, and I can assume I am your current lover exclusively. I do not believe in sharing, and, I trust, neither do you,' he drawled with silken emphasis. 'Or did I get that wrong?'

'No—yes.' He was staring down at her with dark, almost angry eyes and Charlie was hopelessly confused. 'I mean, of course you are.'

My God! Jake actually sounded jealous, she realised, although he had no reason to be. She was about to tell him so, and explain Dave was her boss at International Rapid Rescue, but she didn't get the chance.

'Good.' Looping an arm around her waist, he ushered her into the lift. 'Third floor, correct?'

Mildly affronted by his abrupt manner, she asked, 'I thought you had to work today?' She was not a complete pushover, even if she had given Jake that impression.

'A certain lady left me wide awake and aching, so I worked for what was left of the night.'

She smiled up at him, feeling the tension in the arm that held her leaving him. 'Gosh, unable to sleep? That's funny, I slept like a log.'

Her stomach twisted in knots at the thought of Jake aching for her.

'Witch,' he chuckled, and at that moment they reached her floor.

Inexplicably, Charlie felt nervous showing Jake into the apartment. Taking the carrier from his hand, she said, 'Make yourself at home while I put this away,' and dashed for the kitchen before she did something foolish like grabbing him. She didn't want to appear too desperate.

Jake's dark gaze roamed around what was a basic studio apartment. The place was tiny, and it was obviously used for one thing only: the bed.

A tiny living area contained a sofa that faced a television and music centre, and in between a sheepskin rug covered most of the wood floor. An open staircase led up to a gallery that held a large bed and nothing much else except a door that obviously had to lead to the bathroom. The space beneath the stairs housed a desk and computer and a row of bookcases, and that was it.

It confirmed all his worst suspicions: this was a love nest, or a bachelor pad at best. He cursed the crazy impulse that had made him come looking for Charlotte. It was not like him at all. But after a sleepless night, when visions of her exquisite body had tormented him, and he had sat for a few hours at the computer but had not been able to even occupy his mind with work, his curiosity had got the better of him—and, if he was honest, so had his libido. And he had determined to see her again. Big mistake.

He strode across to the window and the view did nothing to improve his mood: the back of a warehouse. Then he noticed the silver photo frame on the window-sill. He picked it up, his dark eyes narrowing on the picture it contained. A tall, burly, fair-haired man, with a slim dark woman at his side and three children kneeling at their feet. Surely Charlotte's last lover could not be a married man?

'That's Dave and his family.' He turned his head at the sound of her voice. She was standing in the kitchen doorway smiling at him.

Jake remained standing by the window, uneasiness clutching at his gut. His hooded dark eyes raked over Charlotte's slender figure and beaming face. She looked totally unashamed, innocent almost, and yet she was using another man's apartment. A married man at that.

'Very nice.' Jake placed the frame back on the table. 'And this apartment is very cosy, but hardly a family home?' he prompted.

'No. Dave has a house in Dorset and only uses this flat when he is in London on business.'

Jake stiffened. She was as good as admitting a married man had been her lover, and it disgusted him. 'Convenient,' Jake said cynically, subjecting her to a hard, steady appraisal. 'For you.'

His relationship with Charlotte had started out straightforwardly enough, as an act of revenge. After last night he should have left it at that.

Charlotte was moving towards him, her incredible eyes wide and guileless as she flashed him a brilliant smile. 'For everyone. Lisa, his wife, loved the place; she said it was a perfect bolt-hole for the pair of them when the children got too much.' She continued walking towards him. 'Come September Joe, the eldest son, is moving in when he starts at university.'

'You know the whole family?' Jake queried, his suspicion of this Dave as the man in her life fading a little.

'Have done almost all my life.' Charlotte stopped beside him and picked up the picture. 'They've been regulars at the hotel for almost twenty years or so. This is an old photo from when the children were young—they're all teenagers now.' An abstracted smile curved her full lips. 'Lisa was a great friend of my mother's, and after her death Lisa and Dave were great to me, a bit like an honorary aunt and uncle. I stayed quite a few times at their home in Dorset.'

Jake draped a casual arm around her shoulder, took the picture from her unresisting fingers and placed it back on the table, his relief intense. She glanced up at him, and looked a little sad, but she was entitled to be. She was like him, alone in the world, and it worried him. As the elusive Dave no longer worried him. He did what he had ached to do from the moment he had seen her again.

Charlie saw his darkening gaze and just had time to be surprised by the oddest flash of relief in his eyes as he bent towards her and gathered her close and took her softly parted lips in a deep, open-mouthed kiss that inflamed all her senses. Her hand reached for his broad shoulders, and her slender fingers threaded up through the sleek black hair as his tongue pursued a subtle exploration of her mouth. He released her lips and she groaned as his tongue found the delicate coils of her ear. His fingers were deftly moving to the buttons of her shirt, releasing them. She had dressed in haste and was braless and his hand took full advantage, pushing aside the soft cotton and cupping her naked breast. Her body leapt in immediate response, a low groan of pleasure escaping her.

'No,' Jake rasped, lifting his head. He saw the desire in her smoky blue eyes, and forced himself to ignore it as he deftly refastened her blouse and hugged her tight. She deserved better than a quick lay. 'Not here, *cara*. I came to take you to lunch.'

'I'm not that hungry.'

'But I am, and the restaurant at my hotel provides very good food.' He eased her away from him, his dark gaze roaming over her lovely face, and lingering on her lips, and his good intentions were shot to hell. 'And excellent room service,' he added huskily.

'Suddenly, I'm starving. And I would love to join you for lunch.' She beamed back at him.

The openness of her smile, the undisguised sensuality in her brilliant eyes, sent a thrill of anticipation running through Jake's veins, and another course of action occurred to him. 'In that case, while I am on a winning streak—you did say you were on holiday, so how about you pack your bags and take advantage of all the amenities of a first-rate hotel suite, including me, for the next couple of weeks, instead of this tiny apartment?'

'Move in with you?' Charlie was shocked, and still reeling from his assault on her senses. She wanted to, but felt she had to demur. 'But we only met two days ago, we hardly know each other.'

'All the more reason. It will give you time to get to know me. And don't worry, I can truthfully declare I am a financially viable, clean-living, totally unattached male. It is a two-bedroom suite and if you prefer you can have your own room.'

'I don't know,' she murmured. A voice of caution in her head was reminding her Jake wasn't offering her happy ever after. He had told her he would never marry. But her feelings for him overpowered every other consideration.

'Yes, you do,' he said confidently. 'The sexual chemistry between us is electric. We both want the same thing, and badly.' Lifting his hand, he brushed his fingers along the edge of her jaw, and Charlie instinctively moved her head like a cat seeking the stroking fingers. 'And you know it,' he said with a throaty chuckle.

She looked up at him, a brief smile curling her mouth, and said softly, 'Your hotel sounds a lot of fun, Jake. I'll go and pack.'

Jake watched the sway of her pert bottom as she walked up the stairs. His body hardened yet again, and he was tempted to follow her. But instead he lowered himself down on the sofa. He felt strange. He had just asked Charlotte to stay with him for two weeks, something he never did with the women in his life. A week-end, yes, maybe, but longer—never. He shook his head. Two impulsive actions in one day; not like him at all.

Ten minutes later Charlie skipped down the stairs, a holdall in her hand. 'Right, I'm ready.'

'That's it?' Jake rose to his feet, his dark eyes narrowing on the single bag she carried. 'I thought you told me you were on holiday for two weeks.'

'I am, but I always travel light.'

'Amazing.'

'Not really,' Charlie said seriously. 'It's just a question of knowing what you need and packing carefully.'

'If you say so,' Jake agreed and, taking her bag and with his other hand in the small of her back, he urged her out of the apartment.

Following Jake into the hotel, Charlie had a moment of panic. She wished her mother or Lisa were still alive so she had someone to talk to—another female to give her advice about the overwhelming emotions she was experiencing and the action she was about to take.

She glanced around the massive foyer, and the people milling around. The clientele were elegantly dressed, and she was terribly conscious of the simplicity of her own attire. Why, oh, why hadn't she changed, or at least done something about her hair instead of leaving it in a childish pony-tail? She glanced at Jake. He had everything: a great body, stunning looks, he oozed sex appeal, and he wore his casual clothes with an elegance that few men could aspire to.

Sensing her disquiet, Jake closed a comforting hand around her arm. 'Not having second thoughts?'

'No. But I look like something the cat dragged in, compared to everyone here. I stand out like a sore thumb.'

A smile touched his mouth. 'You stand out because you are the most beautiful woman here,' he drawled. 'But if you feel uncomfortable there is an easy remedy.'

Before Charlie realised his intention he had led her across the foyer and into a designer boutique. He spoke to the assistant and informed her, 'This is Miss Summerville. I would like you to provide her with anything she needs.' He produced a diamond credit card from his pocket and placed it on the counter before glancing down at Charlie, a cynical edge to his smile. 'Problem solved. Now take your pick, but don't be long. I'm hungry.'

Blue eyes flashing flames, Charlie said through clenched teeth, 'No, thank you.' If they had been alone she would have hit him. He might be comfortable throwing his money around dressing his lady friends, but Charlie had never felt so mortified in her life. Scarlet-faced, she marched out of the shop.

Jake's arm snaked around her waist. 'I appreciate your haste to get me alone, but you were a little rude walking out on that rather charming lady,' he said mockingly as he led her into the lift.

As soon as the doors closed Charlie spun out of his hold. 'Get you alone!' she exclaimed. 'Are you crazy? I walked out because I have never been so embarrassed in my life. I am perfectly capable of buying my own clothes, and paying my own bill.'

One dark brow arched in astonishment. 'Paying the bill? Forget it! You are my guest—and as for embarrassed, *cara*, why? Women expect the man in their bed to buy them gifts and pay the bills. It is nothing to be embarrassed about. I'm not,' he said with a shrug of his broad shoulders.

Charlie stared at him incredulously. 'Then all I can say is you must have bedded some pretty awful women if you believe that claptrap.' She almost laughed at the look of outrage on his handsome face.

'None that were as outspoken as you, that's for sure,' he shot back. 'Next you will be trying to tell me you have never shared a holiday, or even lived with a man and allowed him to pay the bills.'

Charlie opened her mouth to yell, and stopped. His assumption about her lifestyle was partially her fault; she had tried to be more sophisticated than she really was. She glanced briefly up at him through the thick veil of her lashes. His features were impassive, relaxed, and yet she was aware of a tightly leashed primitive passion just below the surface that made her pulse race and her heart begin its familiar pounding. There was nowhere she wanted to be more than in his arms, and in his bed, and she knew if there was any chance at all of extending their relationship longer than a couple of weeks, it had to be with honesty and trust. Something Jake appeared to have very little faith in.

'No, actually, I have not,' she said quietly, raising her eyes to his and adding, 'This is a first for me.'

Her eyes must have given her away as he muttered something thickly in Italian, and reached for her. The doors slid open and he swore, and walked her across the hall and into his suite with unseemly haste.

'You are an incredible woman. You never cease to surprise me,' Jake husked, and he captured her mouth with his own in a deeply passionate kiss.

She could feel the heavy thud of his heart beneath the palms of her hands resting against his chest… Both his arms were around her, pressing her against him, and she felt his body hardening, merging with hers. She trembled as his lips feathered brief, tormenting kisses against her temples and down to the vulnerable curve of her neck.

'*Dio*, I want you,' Jake murmured against her ear, and, sweeping her up in his arms, he carried her into the bedroom.

They spent the rest of Sunday in bed, and all night. By the time Charlie surfaced on Monday morning she was a different woman. No woman ever had a more ardent lover, she was sure, and she had told Jake so, over and over again, fascinated by his big, hard-muscled body as he taught her with skill and eroticism how responsive her own could be.

She stretched languorously on the bed, and watched Jake, who had ten minutes earlier deserted her for the shower, stroll back into the bedroom wearing only a towel slung low on his hips. He had a magnificent body, all golden skin and rippling muscle, and after last night Charlie was no longer too shy to look.

She followed his progress around the room, saw him withdraw a smart grey suit and white shirt from the wardrobe, and smiled at the intimacy of seeing him dress. First the white boxers, then the white shirt and elegant hip-hugging trousers. 'Going somewhere?' she asked, dragging herself up on an elbow and shaking back the tumbled mass of her ash blonde hair from her face. 'That doesn't look the kind of garb for sightseeing.'

Jake turned from the chest of drawers, a rueful smile on his handsome face and a pair of black socks in his hand, and crossed to sit down on the bed beside her. 'I have a meeting this morning. I did warn you, *cara*, I am here on business.' He smiled wryly when he saw the pout of her love-swollen lips, and, lifting his hand, he ran his fingers through her hair. 'And, no, I am not going to kiss you, otherwise I will never make my meeting.'

His deep, dark eyes gleamed down into hers as he added softly, 'After the last eighteen hours maybe you could use a rest—or to do your own tourist thing today. But I want you back here by six. I'll be waiting.' He pressed a brief kiss on the tip of her nose, before bending down to slip on his socks. A moment later he had donned his shoes, jacket and tie, and turned back to look at her.

'You're amazingly quiet, Charlotte.'

'I was just wondering if I should unpack my clothes in the other bedroom,' she teased. She was too happy to be angry with him and anyway he had said originally it would depend on his business obligations, but she wasn't letting him slope off totally scot-free.

'Ah, I might have lied about that,' Jake returned smoothly, his dark eyes lit with amusement smiling down into hers. 'The second bedroom was converted into an office for the duration of my stay, so unless you want to sleep on the desk…' He paused. 'Then again, a desk has distinct possibilities,' he suggested, a wicked gleam in his dark eyes.

Charlie picked up a pillow and threw it at him. 'Shame on you,' she cried and burst out laughing at the bemused expression on his striking face.

'I'll get you for that later.' Placing the pillow on the foot of the bed, he added, 'And that is a promise, so feel afraid, woman.' He sent her a quick blinding smile that took her breath away. Then he was striding out of the room, with the wave of a hand and a, *'Ciao, cara.'*

Charlie didn't go sightseeing; instead she hit the shops, and blew her clothes allowance for the next year because she wanted to look good for Jake. When she returned slightly after six, he was waiting.

'Typical woman: late and couldn't resist shopping,' he said mockingly as she walked in with a handful of carriers.

'But not from the hotel's overpriced boutique, and paid for by me,' she mocked back.

Without a single word of warning strong hands curved under her arms and hauled her hard against a taut male body, a dark head descended and she was kissed senseless. The carriers fell unnoticed to the ground as she linked her arms around his neck. A few hours later they called room service.

And so it continued for the next few days. Pressure of business meant Jake never accompanied her during the day as she roamed around London, visiting all the places of interest that appealed to her, but she didn't mind because she knew she would see him later. But the nights in the privacy of the suite were the best. He had only to look at her in a certain way, and her whole body heated in instant response.

CHAPTER SIX

FRIDAY showed all the signs of being a beautiful spring day, and as she sat dressed in only a bathrobe Charlie wondered what her chances were of getting Jake to share it with her. She looked across the table at him, noting the magnificent broad shoulders clad in a perfectly tailored dark jacket, the white shirt enhancing the bronzed skin of his almost indecently attractive face. She could look at him for ever. He had finished his breakfast and was filling his cup with coffee for the third time. That was something else she had noted about him: he always drank three cups of coffee.

'You drink too much coffee, Jake,' she declared, her eyes sparkling as she held his faintly brooding gaze. 'And you work too hard. If you're not at a meeting you're on the phone or attached to that computer. You need to relax more. Spend the day with me?'

'If I relaxed any more with you, *cara*, I would be in danger of having a heart attack,' he mocked gently, his dark gaze sliding down to where the soft swell of her breasts was exposed by the lapels of her robe, and back to her face.

'I didn't mean that.' Charlie blushed and Jake laughed. 'For your information,' she said firmly, 'I'm going to Kew Gardens to meander around the tropical plants and pretend I'm on a tropical island somewhere.'

'Now, that I can envisage: you on a paradise island wearing only a grass skirt,' he said. 'We'll do that for real when I have time. But, unfortunately, I can't join you today. I do have a huge corporation to run, and thousands of people who depend on me for their livelihood.'

'Very laudable.' His casual remark suggesting they had a future had made her heart sing. 'But you should remember the old adage: "all work and no play makes Jack a dull boy",' she teased with a smile that faded as she saw his dark brows draw together in a frown.

'I was just joking,' she said.

Jake was not amused, mainly because he knew there was some truth in her words. His gaze focused on her features, noting the sudden faint wariness in her eyes, and he felt bad. She gave him everything in bed and out; her enthusiasm for her ridiculous sightseeing tours, and the pleasure she took in explaining them to him, amused him, and he gave little back.

'I know you were, *cara*,' Jake hastened to reassure her. Charlotte had surprised him this last week. He could count on one hand the women he had actually allowed to share his life for more than a weekend. He preferred to wine, dine, and make love to the woman in his life and return to his own bed to sleep.

Charlotte was the exception, probably because she was the least demanding woman he had ever met. She was nothing like the greedy, selfish bitch he had first believed her to be. He hadn't spent a penny on her, and guiltily he realised he had never actually taken her out all week.

He wasn't the type of man who explained his actions, but Charlotte deserved some explanation. 'Before I met you, I had spent the past three months confined to my home in Italy, because my foster-parents were in poor health and needed my constant support. This trip to London is the first of many overdue visits, and in the next few months I must visit America and the Pacific Rim countries, so if I have appeared a little preoccupied with work, that's why. But all that is about to change.'

Charlie almost gasped out loud at the warmth of the smile he bestowed upon her as, rising to his feet, he crossed to where she sat and turned her around in her chair, and, bending slightly, tipped her chin up with one long finger.

'Be back from your jungle adventure early. We have tickets for the theatre tonight and the curtain rises at seven-thirty.' He lied: he had not got tickets, but he would. 'And tomorrow I am completely at your disposal. You can take me where you want.' Straightening up, he added, 'Though I do have a property to check out in the morning. Perhaps we can combine the two.'

His information about his parents, work and the difficulties he'd had in the past few months was a first, and Charlie was delighted. At last Jake was beginning to confide in her. Hugging him around his hips, she tilted back her head, her blue eyes dancing. 'Careful or you might spoil me,' she chided him, and Jake laughed.

'And you be careful where you hug a man.' He took her hands from around his hips and shot her a mocking glance. 'You could give him the wrong idea.'

* * *

She was late. It was almost seven, and she was so looking forward to the theatre. Dashing out of the lift, she opened the door to their suite and stopped.

'Where the hell have you been? We're due at the theatre in thirty minutes.' Jake was standing in the middle of the room, immaculate in a dark evening suit, but with a face like thunder.

'I know, I know,' she wailed. 'But the tube was delayed and I got stuck in the rush hour.'

'The tube? You travelled on the tube? Are you crazy?'

'Not so you would notice, I hope.' She moved towards him and opened her shoulder-bag at the same time. 'It's okay, I'll be ready in fifteen minutes.'

'It is not okay.' She was made aware of the tension in his tall, commanding figure as he grasped her arm. 'The tube is dangerous for a woman on her own. Have you no sense?' Jake demanded, studying her in angry challenge.

'Oh, Jake, come down from your rarefied planet. It's perfectly safe. I've been using it all week, and no one has leapt on me yet.'

'You…all week!' Hooded eyes, glinting strangely, clashed with blue. 'No more tubes, Charlotte. There will be a car and driver at your disposal from now on. It will be a great deal more convenient and, whatever you say, I am not having you exposed to any danger, however slight.'

'Gosh, I never knew you cared,' she remarked with a grin, and saw the shutters fall across his dark eyes as his hand fell from her arm.

'I care for any person in my charge,' he said stiltedly. 'Hurry and dress. We will be late.'

Delving in her shoulder-bag, she lifted out a box. 'Here, this is for you. I got it in the gift shop at Kew Gardens. When I saw it I thought of you.' She placed it in his hand, and caught his look of astonishment as she turned and headed for the bedroom.

Jake looked at the box in his hand as if it were about to explode. Slowly he opened the box. He withdrew the glass globe, and blinked at the beauty of the delicate exotic flower within. He could not remember the last time anyone had given him a gift for no apparent reason, let alone such an exquisitely simple gift, and he was totally humbled.

A quick shower and Charlie was back in the bedroom in a matter of minutes. Slipping on white lace briefs, she withdrew from the wardrobe the dress she had bought on Monday. It had looked glamorous in the shop, pale pink with a bustier bodice and short straight skirt, but now it looked a little too daring to her mind, and she wondered if Jake would like it. She slipped it over her head anyway. Wondering about Jake had become a full-time occupation, and she now wondered if he liked her present as she sat down at the dressing-table and began to apply a light moisturiser to her face.

It was a black orchid petrified in glass as a paperweight, and now she realised why it reminded her of Jake. He was dark and beautiful, like the orchid, and like it, his true feelings were buried deep in a protective layer. But in his case the glass was probably bulletproof. When she had teased him earlier about caring, the familiar shuttered expression had appeared. But was that so surprising, she mused, given his early life? He had lost his mother young, and been on his own for two years, and that must have affected him. And later, when he had thought he had found love, his fiancée had walked out on him. No wonder he had concentrated all his attention on building up a business empire, and put his feelings in cold storage.

A slow, sensual smile curved her warm mouth. Well, perhaps not that cold. Her mind was made up. She loved Jake and it was up to her to chip away at the glass until she prised the loving, caring man she knew he could be free.

Standing up, she ran a comb through her hair—there wasn't time for anything else—and, smoothing the skirt down over her waist and hips, she picked up her shawl and purse and turned towards the door.

Jake was standing where she had left him in the middle of the room, turning the paperweight over and over in his hand. He swung around, his hooded eyes gleaming with a brightness that looked almost like tears.

'You like it.' She smiled, and Jake's reaction was peculiar.

He placed the paperweight on the table and walked slowly towards her. He placed his hands on her shoulders and said in a low voice husky with emotion, 'Thank you for the gift, Charlotte. I will treasure it always.' Very gently he pulled her against his hard body, and lowered his head to hers.

The kiss was like no other kiss they had shared. It was soft and unbearably tender and went on and on. She lifted her free hand to curve around the nape of his neck, but his head lifted and he released her with a small sigh.

'I promised you the theatre and we will be late,' he offered by way of explanation. Taking her pashmina from her hands, he wrapped it around her shoulders. 'You look beautiful, absolutely stunning.' His dark eyes gleamed with amusement and something more sensual. 'But that is one dangerous gown and you are one dangerous lady. And I am not letting you out of my sight.'

They were too late to catch the first act, but were allowed to enter the auditorium for the second act. At the intermission Jake ordered her a glass of champagne. Leaning against the bar, dark eyes gleaming enigmatically down at her, he said, 'So, what do you think of it so far?'

'Honestly?' She quirked an elegant brow at him. 'It would not have made a blind bit of difference if we had seen the first act. The play is totally incomprehensible. And as for the poor young boy with the bandy legs who keeps appearing in what I suppose is a loincloth, but looks like a nappy—what on earth was his mother thinking of putting him on the stage? He could be traumatised for life.'

Jake threw back his head and laughed out loud. 'Brutally honest,' he said. 'But I couldn't have put it better myself. Let's get out of here and find somewhere to eat.'

The following day Charlie left Jake sleeping for a change. She showered and dressed carefully in more new additions to her wardrobe. Natural linen trousers with a matching tooled leather belt hung low on her hips, a figure-hugging camisole almost met the trousers, and a loosely tailored jacket completed the outfit. She left the jacket off, and ordered room service. When the waiter arrived she took the trolley from him and wheeled it into the bedroom.

Sprawled flat on his back across the bed, naked except for the sheet that just about covered his thighs, Jake was a tempting sight, and for a long moment she feasted her eyes on him. Black hair dishevelled and with an early morning shadow darkening his jaw, he looked like a pirate. All he needed was a gold earring, Charlie thought dreamily.

'Are you going to give me that coffee some time today?' One dark eye opened and Charlie nearly jumped out of her skin.

'You're awake.' She pushed the trolley nearer the bed. 'I thought you might like breakfast in bed.'

Jake hauled himself up on one elbow, his dark, sensuous gaze skimming over her face. 'I would if you were going to join me,' he offered lazily.

'No way. Much as I love you, you promised me the day out,' she shot back. 'And I'm holding you to it.'

His eyes darkened and then became hidden beneath the sweep of his lashes, and she realised what she had just said. But she refused to be embarrassed. It was the truth and Jake could accept it, ignore it, or tell her to get lost. She was tired of trying to play by his rules and she wasn't hiding how she felt any more.

'Then pour me a coffee, and I'll be yours in no time at all.' Obviously he was going to ignore her declaration of love, but at least he had not told her to get lost, which was some consolation. She handed him a cup of coffee and left.

Two hours later, Charlie stood on the balcony of a penthouse apartment situated on the bank of the River Thames, and looked around her, absorbing the stunning view of the city spread out before her. She was a country girl at heart but she could certainly get used to this. Her lips twitched in the beginnings of a smile as she turned to go back inside. Fat chance.

She walked across to where Jake was leaning over a table, studying a blueprint. 'Are you really going to buy this apartment?' she asked.

'Actually, I was thinking more of the whole building.' Jake cast her a sidelong glance and straightened to his full height. 'It's an excellent long-term investment. But as it happens, this apartment is available, and it might be useful to have a permanent base in London.' He lifted an enquiring brow. 'What do you think?'

'I love it.' She felt flattered he had asked her opinion. 'But then, I'm not in your league when it comes to business.'

'It wasn't business I was thinking of.' Reaching an arm around her waist, he pulled her to him. 'But from a woman's point of view, would you rather spend time with a man here?' His eyes glinted when he saw her blush. 'Or in a hotel?'

'If it was the man I loved, it wouldn't matter,' Charlie responded honestly, her sapphire eyes holding his.

They stared mutely at one another for a long moment, and Jake was the first to break the contact. His arm fell from her waist and he took a step back to lean against the table. 'A typical romantic response. You must know very little about your own sex if you believe that.' She was struck by the sudden cold glitter in his dark eyes. 'Take it from me, most women will run a mile if the man in their life doesn't support them in the manner to which they would like to be accustomed.'

'That is a sweeping generalisation,' she said. 'And I don't believe it for a minute.'

'Try telling that to my ex-fiancée. She took off like lightning when she realised I wasn't as wealthy as she had thought.'

'That must have hurt,' Charlie murmured.

'No.' Jake took in a controlled breath. 'Her leaving did not hurt at all, and how in the hell did we get onto this subject?' He shook his head and wrapped a strong, lean hand around Charlie's wrist, which he twisted around her back, pulling her in close to his great body. His other hand came up and touched her smooth cheek. 'What is it about you that makes me tell you things I don't mean to?'

'My fatal charm,' she replied cheekily. She had learnt more about Jake over the last few days and understood a lot better now why he appeared so hard-headed and controlled.

'You could be right at that,' Jake husked, his dark head bending. Her lips involuntarily parted for his kiss, but instead he whispered in her ear, 'You can prove it later.' He dropped his fingers from her cheek to rest on her hip, his dark eyes laughing down at her. 'As it happens, I already bought this place yesterday. Come on, the rest of the day is for you.'

They spent it at London Zoo and Charlie, with her arm linked through Jake's, for the first time felt as if they were a normal couple. They laughed at the monkeys, and she shivered at the snakes while Jake held her close. They ate sandwiches outside the café in the zoo, and when Charlie fell in love with a soft cuddly panda in the gift shop, Jake bought the toy for her. Much later they dined on scampi and chips sitting outside a pub on the river. Jake was convinced that whatever was in the popular English dish had never been in the sea, and they were still light-heartedly arguing on the merits of Italian versus English food when they returned to the hotel. Finally Charlie threw her hands up and admitted that Italian cuisine won hands down, and Jake took advantage of her position to whip her top over her head…

Sometimes Charlie had to pinch herself to believe he was real, and she told him so early on the Friday of the second week.

Jake laughed lazily, and told her to feel him and make sure. She did, all over. And he called her a natural-born sensualist, and made wild, passionate love to her, until she thought she would lose her mind with the excitement of his powerful body driving her to the edge of sense and beyond.

Exhausted, they lay sprawled together on the bed. She said in a breathless voice, 'Now I know why I love you. And I'm totally convinced you're real.' She spread her fingers through the damp hair on his chest, feeling the rapid pounding of his heart beneath her palm. She heard him chuckle and she pulled gently on the short, curling body hair.

'Find me funny, do you?' she teased. But the telephone rang on the bedside table before he could respond. She watched as he lifted the receiver, and said something in Italian. She felt his body tense, and heard the change of tone in his rich deep voice, even though she could not understand what he was saying.

Ending the call, Jake sprang off the bed, and glanced down at her. 'That was my office in Italy. I have to leave immediately.' Without another word, he headed for the bathroom.

Stunned, she stared at his broad back as he disappeared into the bathroom. She loved Jake and he was leaving. It had to happen eventually, she knew, but blindly she had pushed the knowledge to the back of her mind, not wanting to face reality. Now she had no choice.

Well, what had she expected, for heaven's sake? she asked herself. Jake had a huge corporation to run, and her manager was expecting her back on Sunday. So Jake had to leave a day earlier than planned. It was no big deal. She would see him again.

Jake strolled back into the room. 'Okay.' He tossed her a brief glance, and proceeded to dress with the same brisk efficiency he did everything.

Charlie had watched him countless times before, but somehow this morning she couldn't. She was too afraid of betraying her misery at his imminent departure. Jumping off the bed, she crossed to the walk-in wardrobe, selected navy trousers and a blue ribbed sweater, then collected fresh underwear and stepped into the bathroom.

Standing in the shower, she told herself not to overreact. If the last two weeks had proved anything, it was that they were great together. She loved him and she felt it in her bones that Jake cared about her. They were both mature adults with busy careers; it was natural they would be apart sometimes.

As she walked into the lounge ten minutes later she was still telling herself she had nothing to worry about.

Jake was standing by the table, leafing through some papers in a briefcase, the expression on his face one of intense concentration. The suitcases by his side told her he had already packed. He was dressed in a dark pinstriped business suit, white shirt and grey silk tie, and he looked every inch the hard-headed tycoon. But she knew the other Jake, the passionate tender lover, and a sob caught in her throat at the thought of him leaving.

She must have made some sound because his dark head lifted and she walked across to him. 'You're already packed.'

'Yes.' Jake placed a brief, somewhat distracted kiss on her cheek. 'I'm sorry I have to leave so quickly, but my presence is required in Italy.'

'I know. But it's a shame we are going to lose our last day together.' She couldn't prevent the slight tremble of her lips.

Jake placed a finger over her mouth. 'There will be other days, Charlotte. I'll call you tonight. Stay here and enjoy your last day.'

Her pleasure at his promise to call her was dented by his suggestion she stay on at the hotel. To be here alone held no appeal. 'No, I wouldn't feel comfortable staying here without you. I'll go home.'

'Whatever you want,' he said gruffly. Suddenly a conscience that had never troubled Jake before where women were concerned reared its head. He was the 'love them and leave them' type, the women suitably rewarded of course, but Charlotte was different. Sure, he had lusted after her, but his original intention had been less than honourable and he prided himself on being an honourable man.

He couldn't just walk away from her. So he did something he never did: he wrote a number on the back of a business card. 'This is my home number in Genoa. If you need me, call me. And now I really must go—the jet is waiting.'

Charlie watched him snap shut his briefcase, blinking back the tears.

'Already?' The tremble in her voice gave her away.

'Afraid so.' The bellboy arrived to take the suitcases and Jake brushed a brief kiss against her trembling lips and left.

Dr Jones had been Charlie's GP all her life. He dined at the hotel restaurant regularly, and quite often Charlie joined him: he was more friend than doctor. But looking at him now, she was horrified.

'You're sure?' she asked for the third time.

'Yes, Charlie dear. From the date you have given me, you are almost seven weeks pregnant.'

'But we used protection,' she murmured, shaking her head in disbelief.

'Obviously not enough,' Dr Jones said dryly. 'But it isn't the end of the world. You're pregnant, not ill; you're a very fit young woman, Charlie, and I know you will have a beautiful, healthy baby. So I'm sure you have nothing to worry about. Go home and tell the lucky man.'

Easier said than done, Charlie thought, staring blindly at the pile of invoices on the desk in front of her three days later.

'It's no good sitting daydreaming, Charlie.'

At the sound of her manager Jeff's voice, her head lifted. 'I am not dreaming,' she snapped. 'I'm trying to work.'

'If you say so.' Jeff stopped by the desk and looked down at her, compassion in his grey eyes. 'You should tell the father. He has a right to know. It's not like you to shirk your responsibilities.'

Jeff had known Charlie since she was twelve, when he had been hired by her grandfather to manage the hotel. She had been a bright, lively child, a joy to all who knew her, and he hated to see her so miserable.

'This baby is my responsibility, and what I would like to know is, how the hell did all the staff find out I was pregnant the same day it was confirmed?' Charlie demanded, running a hand distractedly through her blonde hair.

'Maybe because you came back from your holiday, glowing like a woman in love, you mentioned Jake d'Amato just once or twice and bought a "Teach Yourself Italian" book. So when you started dashing off to be sick every day, it was a bit of a give-away. Plus everyone knew you had a doctor's appointment,' Jeff said with a chuckle. 'They all care about you, and most of them guessed you were pregnant long before you realised what was up.'

'Thanks! Thanks very much! So not only does everyone in the hotel know I'm pregnant, they think I'm a pregnant idiot for not recognising the signs.' Charlie groaned. 'What am I going to do?'

'I've told you. Ring the man, and do it now. I have to go and fill in on the desk. Amy was supposed to be on Reception but she has an optician's appointment. I'll catch you later. Do it,' Jeff reiterated, walking out the door.

The trouble was, Charlie thought forlornly, she already had called Jake's home near Genoa three times since the doctor had confirmed her pregnancy, hoping to get a message to him, but she had only managed to speak to some woman called Marta, whose English was as bad as Charlie's Italian.

In the five weeks since she had last seen Jake, her tentative belief that he might love her as she loved him had taken a severe jolt. He'd rung to make sure she'd arrived back home safely, and then nothing for a week. Then he'd called to tell her he was going to America and would get in touch when he got back. She had heard nothing since, but had lived on hope and consoled herself with the fact she knew he was in America.

But yesterday, leafing through a magazine one of the departing guests had left behind, she had seen a double-page spread of a prestigious charity dinner in New York, and staring out from one picture was Jake d'Amato with a stunning brunette at his side. According to the item accompanying the picture, Jake's companion was Melissa, a model and long-time 'friend' of Jake, better known for her string of wealthy lovers than her modelling career.

Charlie hadn't tried to call Jake again. Face it, she told herself sadly, she had been taken for a fool. While she had fallen in love, to Jake she had been nothing more than a passing fancy. She blinked back the tears that moistened her eyes. She was not going to cry. She had done enough of that in the past few weeks and she had to stop.

She should have known a man like Jake d'Amato was far too sophisticated to be attracted by a naive virgin for long. Remembering the last day when they had parted, she knew she had felt him withdrawing from her. He had been cool and his kiss goodbye had been little more than a peck. In fact, when Charlie thought about it now, the only thing that was surprising was that he had bothered to call her at all!

Anger and pain bubbled up inside her. In every other area of her life she was super-efficient. She could run a hotel, climb a rock-face, or search for the dead and dying in any catastrophe around the world. She was compassionate by nature and slow to anger. Yet in the male-female stakes she was an absolute novice.

Morosely, she concluded falling in love was heaven and hell. In her case mostly hell: the butterflies in the stomach, the hunger, the need for one man and the constant doubt as to whether Jake felt the same. Well, it was all going to change. She had been acting like a lovesick fool long enough.

Angrily she brushed her hand across her eyes and, shoving back the chair, she stood up, squaring her slender shoulders. No man was going to take her for a mug and get away with it, she vowed. In fact… Impulsively she grabbed the telephone and pressed out a number she knew by heart. She heard the *'Pronto,'* through a red mist of anger, and burst into speech. She didn't care if Marta only understood one word in ten. Charlie was going to have her say.

'Tell that no-good bastard you call a boss, I am pregnant and he is going to be a father. *Charlotte incinta, Jake papà—capisco?*' She sarcastically inserted the few Italian words she knew, regardless of grammar, and slammed the phone down.

Whether they made sense or Marta understood, Charlie didn't care. It had made her feel a hell of a lot better. Plus, she thought as she left her office, she could tell Jeff quite honestly she had done the right thing and told the father, and get him off her back.

'I could cover Amy's shift for you, Jeff,' she offered, stopping at the reception desk. With the hotel booked solid for the summer, the staff were at full stretch, and Charlie was adept at filling in when the need arose.

'No, I'm fine. Why don't you take the day off? You've hardly been out of the place in weeks. The sun is shining and Dave and his brood are going sailing for the day. Chef is preparing a picnic. I'll tell him to add a few of your favourites and you can join them. It will do you the world of good.'

Jeff was right. She had hung around the hotel day and night like an idiot waiting for the phone to ring, hoping Jake would call. Well, not any more. She had another human being to worry about now.

'You're right as usual, Jeff,' she admitted with a wry self-mocking smile. 'I have been behaving like an idiot.'

'You, an idiot? Never.' A laughing voice floated over her shoulder. Charlie spun around and smiled at the big, burly grey-haired man grinning down at her. Dave had obviously just left the dining room, with his brood: Joe, eighteen, James, sixteen, and Mary, two years behind. 'You are a pearl among women, and if you would help me control this lot for the day, I'll even put it in writing,' he teased.

A day sailing was a far better prospect than moping around the hotel another minute. 'Yes, okay, Dave.' The fresh air and the company of good friends was just what she needed to help her banish the depressing thoughts about Jake. 'I'll go and change and meet you at the jetty in twenty minutes.'

* * *

'Come on, Charlie,' the boys yelled. 'The water's great, it's not like you to be the last in.'

Wearing a black bikini and stretched out on a towel placed on the fore deck of the sailing boat, Charlie was feeling surprisingly content. She grinned and waved a lazy hand. 'No, I've eaten far too much, maybe later.'

They had sailed to the southern end of the lake, and dropped anchor at a favourite little cove to have their picnic. The three teenagers all had healthy appetites, and Charlie had been no slouch.

'Very wise.' Dave flopped down beside her. 'You have to be careful in your condition.'

'Oh, God!' Charlie groaned. 'Not you as well. You only arrived yesterday, for heaven's sake. Surely the bush telegraph isn't that fast?'

'Afraid so. Jeff told me over a couple of beers last night. He thought I should know as your team leader and more importantly as your friend, Charlotte.' Charlie knew she was in for a lecture when Dave used her full name. 'You know of course you're off the International Rapid Rescue now, but finding a replacement of your calibre is not my main worry. You are, Charlie. I've known you since the first time Lisa and I came here on holiday almost twenty years ago, and you are as dear to me as my family. And Lisa would say the same if she was still alive,' he said seriously.

She had known she would have to give up the team, but it was the sentiment Dave had expressed that made Charlie blink the sudden moisture from her eyes. Lisa and Dave had visited the hotel with their expanding family for almost as long as she could remember. And she knew how hard Lisa's death from breast cancer last year had hit Dave and the children. 'Thank you for that,' she murmured.

'Yes, well, the thing is, I can't help feeling responsible for the condition you're in. If—'

'You are certainly not responsible. I think I'd know if I had slept with you,' she cut in with a cheeky grin, trying to lighten the atmosphere.

'Forget the jokes, Charlotte, this is serious. If I had never said you needed a change of scene and offered you the use of the studio, maybe you'd never have met the man who has been careless enough to make you pregnant. But that aside, the important question is, do you love each other?'

There was no point in denying the truth. Dave knew her far too well and would see through a lie in a second. 'I love Jake, but I doubt he loves me,' she said flatly.

'According to Jeff, the man is some kind of industrial tycoon who lives abroad. But you do keep in touch with him? Whether he loves you or not, you have to tell him you're pregnant. It is natural for you to have doubts in your condition, but you will probably be pleasantly surprised. Trust me, I know my own sex. Any man would be ecstatic to have a woman like you for his wife and the mother of his children.'

'Yes, sure,' she agreed dryly. At that point three very wet teenagers flopped on the deck and ended the adult conversation, much to Charlie's relief, for the rest of the afternoon.

It was late, almost six, when they finally tied the boat up at its mooring. The teenagers yelled, 'Race you to the hotel!' and set off at a run.

'Ah, to be thirty years younger,' Dave groaned.

Charlie flashed him a grin and raced off after the others. The day on the water had done her the world of good, but she was tired and finally had to stop and catch her breath. She looked up at the hotel with the backdrop of the woods embracing it. The grey stone walls gleamed in the evening sun, the immaculate garden stretched down to where she stood with the lake behind her, and she thought she had never seen the old place look more beautiful.

A bittersweet smile curved her soft lips. She was almost home. She placed her hand over her still flat stomach in a tender gesture of reassurance to her unborn child. 'Whatever else happens in life, you and I will always have a home here,' she said with a deep sigh of contentment.

The day out had cleared her head. She was expecting Jake d'Amato's baby, and already she loved them both. But she knew better than most there were no guarantees in life. She had lost all her family, and she had seen through her work generations of families destroyed, even whole towns. She was pregnant, and she now had the chance to build her own little family. Charlie knew with absolute certainty that she had the ability and the strength of will to give her child a good life. As for Jake, she loved him and probably always would, but whether they got together was no longer the main issue. Her baby was her first concern, now and always.

'Age catching up with you too?' Dave quipped as he reached her, and placed a guiding hand around her waist. 'Come on, I'll help you up the hill.'

Charlie laughed. 'Shouldn't that be the other way around, old man?'

The Lakeview Hotel was a beautiful old building, in a magnificent setting and not at all what Jake had expected. It had to be over a hundred years old, and constructed in stone with an elegant terrace along the front. The interior was Victorian in style with stone-mullioned windows, and mahogany-panelled walls, the wood mellowed with the patina of years. He doubted if the place had changed much since it was built, and, glancing at the key rack while waiting for the receptionist, he noted there were only twenty letting rooms. Hardly a big enough hotel to make much of a profit. Not surprising Charlotte was eager to contact him, he thought cynically.

He had begun to believe in the two weeks they had spent together she was not the greedy, selfish bitch he had first thought. But now he realised she was cleverer than most. She had been aiming for the jackpot, a meal ticket for life. Impatiently he drummed his fingers on the desk. Where the hell was the receptionist?

A tall thin man finally appeared. 'Can I help you, sir?'

'Yes, I want to see the owner. Charlotte Summerville,' Jake snapped. He wasn't used to waiting.

'Your name, sir?'

'Jake d'Amato. She knows who I am,' he said impatiently.

'I am the manager—perhaps I can help?'

Jake looked at him and caught a look of amusement in the pale eyes. 'No, you damn well can't. I want to see Charlotte.' He was furious and he was taking no insolence from any man. 'Tell her I'm here.'

'That might be difficult, sir, as she has gone sailing for the day. We are expecting her about six.' Jake glanced at his watch. He would have to cool his heels for over an hour. 'If you would care to wait, I'll have the waitress serve you tea.'

There was no point in arguing—it wasn't the manager he was mad at. Taking a seat in the lounge, he suffered the attentions of a stony-faced waitress. He drank tea, which he loathed, and got the distinct impression from the cold looks slanted his way by the members of staff who passed by that they actively disliked the guests. Or perhaps it was just him in particular. Well, he had had enough. Slapping the paper he had been trying to read down on the table, Jake rose to his feet and strode towards the double doors leading to the garden and beyond.

Three teenagers were running towards him, laughing and shouting, and he quickly stepped up onto the terrace that fronted the hotel. Where the hell was Charlotte? he wondered, gazing out over the glorious gardens to the lake beyond, and then he saw her.

Clad in the briefest of white shorts and a cropped top, she looked incredibly beautiful. Her long blonde hair, glinting with platinum streaks in the evening sun, tumbled around her shoulders and her long legs moved with lithe grace as she ran towards him.

A brilliant smile of pure masculine satisfaction cut across Jake's strong face. She still adored him. He forgot he was furious. Five long weeks he had been without her—he must have been mad to wait so long. But not any more and a charge of testosterone fired up his body with incredible excitement. Then she stopped.

In the next second Jake realised he could swing from euphoria to a fury that threatened to explode as the truth hit him like a blow to the solar plexus. She was not running towards him, she had not even seen him, and she was not alone. From his vantage point, with his grip white-knuckled on the terrace balustrade, he watched Charlotte laugh happily up into the face of the older man who had stopped beside her, and, with an ease born of long practice, slipped an arm around her bare waist.

Jake jerked his proud head back, and drew in a sharp lungful of air. No man touched his woman, not ever. Outraged and furious beyond belief he vaulted over the balustrade and strode towards her.

Charlie, in blissful ignorance of the impending confrontation, was happily regaling Dave with details of her trip around Kew Gardens when Dave interrupted her, his arm falling from her.

'Don't look now, but a very large, very dark and very angry man has just leapt off the terrace and is heading our way.'

Charlie's head spun to the front. Jake! It was Jake in the flesh, and a quivering excitement lanced through her, quickly followed by a shiver of something very like fear. She could feel the anger, the fury sizzling from him at twenty paces.

'Charlotta. At last,' he drawled, his black molten gaze capturing hers as he closed the distance between them, hauled her into his arms, and crushed her against his broad chest. 'I came at your call, *cara*.' His deep accented voice resounded in her ear, and for a split second she remained frozen. Then she trembled helplessly, the familiar wild excitement rushing through her veins as he angled his head and took her slightly parted lips, probing straight between them with a savage, possessive passion that left her breathless and weak at the knees when he finally ended the kiss.

Heavy-lidded black eyes gleamed steadily down at her flushed face and slightly swollen mouth. 'You missed me…yes?' he prompted.

Charlie nodded her head. Jake was here, and he still wanted her.

'Good. Then perhaps you would care to introduce me to your companion.' He recognised the man from the photograph, but Jake had a point to make.

'My companion?' Charlie was not thinking straight; in fact she was having trouble thinking at all. She lifted puzzled eyes to his face, and was taken aback to discover he was looking coolly over her head. Only then did she remember Dave. She turned brick-red and tried to ease out of Jake's hold, but he was having none of it. Instead he simply spun her around, one strong arm curved across her bare waist trapping her back against his chest.

His free hand he offered towards Dave, his blatantly possessive masculine stance saying clearer than words that she was his woman. 'Jake d'Amato, and you are?'

Cool and calm, Dave took the extended hand. 'Dave Watts. A very old friend of the family and a kind of honorary dad to Charlie since the death of her parents.'

'Really. I trust not of the sugar variety.'

'Definitely not,' Dave said bluntly. 'But I can see why you would be worried. She is very sweet.'

Charlie was shocked at Jake's outrageous comment and she felt the sudden tension in his body. Twisting her head, she glanced up at him. His dark eyes were narrowed with piercing intensity on Dave, and, twisting back, she saw Dave was equally intense. They resembled nothing so much as two great predatory beasts meeting head to head before fighting to the death.

Then it struck her. Jake's passionate kiss had been arrogant macho posturing at the sight of Dave. Jake didn't love her, but his massive ego would not allow him to entertain the thought she might have another man. Simmering with resentment, she watched in silence as the two men eyeballed each other. Then suddenly Dave laughed out loud.

'You'll do.' He slapped Jake on the back as if they had been friends for years. 'But hurt her and you'll have me to reckon with. And now I better go and chase up the boys, before they cause any damage. See you later, Charlie.' And he walked away.

She'd been unwilling to cause a scene in front of Dave, but Charlie had no such qualms when he left. 'Let go of me, you big jerk,' she snapped and twisted violently in Jake's hold.

'Certainly.' Jake spun her around to face him. 'But first, tell me, where is Dave's wife? He seems overly protective of you as a happily married man,' he demanded, all hard male arrogance.

'Lisa died last year,' Charlie said flatly. 'And before you insinuate Dave is my lover, let me tell you not all men have the morals of a sewer rat.'

'Implying I have?' Jake drawled. He was an astute judge of character, and he knew his own sex well. The arm Dave had had around Charlotte's waist had not been avuncular, and given half a chance Dave would take it. But not any more. Jake had made that plain. As for Charlotte…his intense dark eyes swept over her beautiful face. She looked the picture of innocence, but then she always had looked innocent. It was the first thing he had noticed about her at the art gallery before he had seen her cynical smile and dismissive shake of her head when viewing the painting and dismissed it as play-acting. But then she had also felt innocent, he recalled, as the first time they had made love flashed in his mind. Her startled gasp, her incredible hot, tight body was not a good image to remember when he was already rigid with desire, and, dropping his arm from her waist, he stepped back. He adjusted his suit jacket and stuck his hands into the pocket of his tailored trousers, his fingers curling into fists.

The jury was still out on Charlotte. The fury that had engulfed him when Marta had passed on Charlotte's message this morning and fuelled his immediate flight to England was still simmering.

'If the cap fits,' Charlie sneered, lifting stormy blue eyes to his, and was even more incensed. Jake was so suave, so in control. He was immaculately clad in a tailored slate-grey business suit, and he should have looked incongruous in the casual setting, but he didn't. He looked magnificent, swaying back on his heels waiting…and watching.

The silence lengthened, and the tension. Biting her lips, she reined in her temper. 'What are you doing here, Jake?'

She was no fool. His passionate embrace on arriving had been nothing more than his high-handed way of manipulating her feelings in front of Dave. But no matter how hurt and suspicious she was, she still wanted Jake. She had ached and cried over him for five painful weeks, in a roller-coaster ride of emotions, ecstatic when he called and plagued with doubt when he didn't. Ashamed of her weakness, she tilted her chin. 'Apart from insulting my friend, that is.'

Jake studied her with fixed attention, his dark eyes gleaming below thick black lashes. He wondered if she had any idea how desirable she looked, her lovely face flushed with anger and her chin tilted at a defiant angle. 'I don't wish to argue with you over your friend.'

'I bet you don't,' Charlie mocked, the picture in the magazine still fresh in her mind. Jake was a two-timing snake. 'Enjoy yourself in New York, did you? I hear you met up with your *old friend* Melissa,' she snarled and watched as his black brows drew together in a frown.

'You saw the magazine article,' he said, with a smug smile dawning that made her want to knock it off his face.

'Dinner good, was it? Or was the smile on your face for the afters you were anticipating?'

'Very good, and it was for a very good cause,' Jake said silkily. Charlotte was jealous and, much as he was tempted to play her along, there were more important matters at stake here. 'Melissa *is* an old friend, and, yes, before you ask, we were lovers, but it was over months before I met you. She left me for another wealthy man who, as it happens, was her date at the dinner—not I.'

'She left you!' Charlie exclaimed. Furious with the man, she still found it incredible that any woman would willingly dump Jake d'Amato.

He shrugged. 'It was no big deal. A mutual parting of the ways.' Charlie was inclined to believe him, because she knew from personal experience Jake was a workaholic and she doubted any woman was a big deal to him, including herself. 'But enough about my past love life. It is the present I am here to talk about, and preferably not in public view.'

Only then was Charlie aware there were a few guests strolling around the garden. She went from outraged anger to mortification in one second flat.

'Unless of course you would like everyone in the hotel to know you are pregnant. After all, you had no hesitation in telling my housekeeper before me. That is why you called me, isn't it?' he demanded curtly.

Fiery colour burned her cheeks. Her Italian must have been better than she thought. Jake knew she was pregnant. As if that were not bad enough, so did almost everyone in the hotel, and she had a horrible suspicion that if Jake ever discovered he was the last to find out, he was not going to be delighted.

'I—I—uh, yes. And it seems like a good idea to talk in private,' she said, her huge eyes studiously avoiding his. 'If you'll follow me, my home is around the back. Over there, the west wing, actually.'

CHAPTER SEVEN

CHARLIE heaved a sigh of relief when they finally reached the safety of her sitting room without encountering anyone. 'Would you like a drink? Tea or coffee?' She headed for the kitchen, and turned. 'Or something stronger,' she suggested politely. Jake was standing in the middle of the room, big, dark and threatening.

'No, thank you. I've had a stomach full of your English tea.' By the grim glance he gave her, he'd had enough of her as well.

Charlie ran clammy hands down her shorts, hovering in the kitchen doorway, uncertain what to do next. Her shock and delight at his arrival had quickly changed to fury and finally embarrassment. She should never have made that phone call. 'I—I take it you got my message,' she said, swallowing nervously, her heart beating like a drum in her chest.

'Yes.' His dark eyes didn't leave her face as he moved to stop a few inches in front of her. 'Interesting, Charlotte: your knowledge of Italian has improved enough to tell my housekeeper you are pregnant, and I am going to be a papa. Not something I appreciated,' he said through gritted teeth. 'Nor having to disturb my pilot on a Sunday and fly halfway across Europe to discover the truth.'

She had never seen him so angry. It was in every line of his big taut body, intimidating in its intensity. 'You could have just phoned,' Charlie murmured when he continued to stand and stare grimly at her, and she lowered her eyes, unable to meet the hard censure in his.

The call had been foolish, she knew, but then she had been hurting badly. She had told him she loved him, laid her heart on the line in the hope he cared, and yet he had not called her for a month—and to see a picture of him in a magazine with another woman… She had flipped. Her hunger for him was an ever-present ache; the longing to see his rare brilliant smile, to hear his voice, to touch him, haunted her dreams.

'No, I could not,' he said. 'A phone call wouldn't do for me. I want to be looking into your eyes when you tell me I am going to be a father.' His dark eyes narrowed to angry slits, and he caught her chin with a thumb and finger and forced her to look at him. 'Are you pregnant, Charlotte?'

'Yes, I am,' she said bluntly. She was thrilled and excited at the prospect, but also frightened, and she wanted nothing more than for Jake to take her in his arms and tell her it would be all right. But by the look on his face she doubted he would.

'And just when did you fall pregnant?' he demanded roughly.

'Seven weeks ago.' She still had not got over the shock that she had got pregnant the first or second time she had made love. 'How unlucky is that?' Charlie didn't realise she had spoken her thought out loud until his hand fell abruptly from her chin and he stepped back and looked at her as if she were contaminated. She saw the humourless smile that twisted his firm lips and flinched at the venom in it.

'Unlucky?' His dark eyes held tightly leashed rage. 'For me, maybe, but damned convenient for you. Amazingly, it is exactly how long we have known each other.'

Jake was madder than hell. It was so obvious: she had put him squarely in the frame as the father…but was he? No woman had enraged and inflamed him as comprehensively as

Charlotte. He had tried to put her out of his mind, but his body would not let him, a galling admission to make, but not one he intended to act on. His dark eyes raked assessingly over her. The tiny white shorts hugged her hips like a second skin, and her stomach still appeared flat, but perhaps her breasts were a little fuller… No! He didn't want to go there. Yes, he did. But he had no intention of being conned by a blue-eyed little gold digger, however desirable, his hard eyes sweeping back up to her lovely face.

'Isn't it rather early to have a pregnancy confirmed?' he queried with biting cynicism. 'Unless the woman in question is eager to get pregnant.'

'Not if you are as sick as a chip every day for three weeks,' she flashed, looking up at him, and stopped. 'You don't believe me,' she said slowly. She could see it in his eyes, in the cynical curl of his lips. She shook her head, and, turning away from him, she crossed to the sofa and collapsed onto it, folding her arms around her waist, suddenly cold. It had never occurred to her Jake wouldn't believe her.

'I never said that,' he pointed out, following her.

'You didn't need to,' she flared back at him. She could see the anger in every tense line of his body, hear it in every word he spoke. The Jake she loved, the Jake she thought she knew, was not this furious stranger towering over her.

'Can you blame me? You would not be the first woman to try and trap a wealthy husband with a mythical pregnancy. I want proof.'

A wealthy...proof... Charlie heaved in a shuddering breath. She was slow to anger, but this arrogant man standing before her had succeeded in doing just that. Jake had arrived at her home unannounced, insulted her and her friend, and then had the colossal nerve to suggest she was lying and was only after his money.

Fury made her leap up from the sofa and stand glaring at him. 'Call yourself a man?' she derided, her eyes flashing blue flame. 'You sleep with me for a fortnight and then string me along with a couple of calls, ignore me for a month, and then you come charging over here in your private jet, full of self-righteous rage. Terrified I might cost you *money*,' she said with enough scorn to make him clench his fists at his sides to control his anger. 'Demanding proof I'm pregnant.' Shaking with rage, she shoved him in the chest with the flat of her hand, and his mouth tightened to a thin line, but he let her. 'What do you suggest?' she demanded hysterically. 'I slash my belly open to show you? Is that it, is that what you really want—a convenient termination? Is that cheap enough for you?'

Jake's cool façade cracked wide open and he paled like a man in shock. 'No. *Dio*, no.' His strong hands reached out to grasp her shaking shoulders and he pulled her to him, his face only inches from her own. 'Don't say that, Charlotte, don't even think it.' His black eyes, wide with horror, were fixed on hers, his fingers biting into her flesh.

Shocked out of her near hysterics by the force of his reaction, she snapped, 'Don't worry, I have every intention of keeping my child. And let go of me, you're hurting me.'

Jake drew in a deep, audible breath. 'I didn't realise.' His hands gentled on her shoulders, but he did not let her go.

Which was just as well because Charlie suddenly felt weak. 'What a disaster,' she murmured. Her hormones were all over the place, and the emotional turmoil of the past few weeks was finally getting to her. And discovering the father of her child thought she was after his money didn't help. The only positive was Jake had made it very clear he didn't want her to terminate the pregnancy.

'It does not have to be a disaster,' Jake said. 'I will marry you.'

Her head jerked up. 'Marry—? If that was a proposal it lacked something in the offering,' she said bluntly. 'I am having this baby, and, I can assure you, living as I do, I am in an ideal position to bring up my own child.' She was being perverse, she knew. Jake was offering her everything she had ever dreamed of, and half an hour ago she would have jumped at the chance, but now she was no longer so sure. She had never heard him so angry or so insulting.

Jake stiffened, his hands dropping from her shoulders, and suddenly he was back to his cool, arrogant best, all trace of emotion gone, more like the Jake she knew so well. 'Don't be ridiculous. There is nothing ideal about bringing up a child without a father. Believe me, I know. So we will get married as soon as it can be arranged.'

He was right, she knew. So why was she so reluctant? Because she wanted it all: she wanted

Jake to love her, as she loved him. Was she being unreasonable?

'You know it makes sense,' he prompted. His dark eyes meshed with hers, and something in the glittering depths made her heart twist. 'What I said before about being trapped into marriage, I didn't mean it—not with you, never with you. But I was shocked and mad at the way I heard the news, and reacted badly.'

'Very,' she said dryly, but she could understand. Telling his housekeeper had been a bit over the top.

'The two weeks we were together were the happiest I have spent in my life,' he said, and Charlie felt a glimmer of hope ignite in her heart. 'We are good together.' He lifted a finger and trailed it gently down her cheek. 'You know we are, better than good. Marry me. You know you want to.' His hand slipped down to curve her waist and his hand on her naked flesh sent a shiver down her spine.

Jake was the only man in the world for her and, with his eyes still locked to hers, the warmth in them unmistakable, she wondered why she was arguing with him. He was offering her everything she ever wanted. If only he could say the word *love*.

Then he broke the eye contact and his hand moved to rest on her flat stomach, a slow smile curving his wide mouth. 'I take it the child is mine. Not that it matters.'

Fury swept through her again and she batted his hand away. 'Yes, it damn well is!' She glared at him, her eyes wild with outrage. 'You are the only man I was ever dumb enough to sleep with in my life, and look where that got me!' she snarled, mortally offended he even needed to ask.

She felt him tense and saw a gleam of incredible emotion in his dark eyes before long lashes lowered, masking his expression. 'All the more reason why you should marry me,' he argued. 'You find me irresistible among men.' A sudden rare brilliant smile illuminated his extraordinarily handsome features. 'You love me.'

'Sex, that's all it was,' Charlie shot back. 'You conceited jerk, that's all I was…' She stopped, as the last of his insulting question registered. *Not that it matters.* He had said—Jake was prepared to marry her unconditionally. He must love her even if he could not say the words.

'No,' Jake denied. 'It was never just sex with you and me.'

An image flashed before him of Charlotte naked in the shower their first night together, her legs wrapped around his waist, her eyes wide and incredulous as he had surged into her sleek, silken body without a thought of protection. And earlier, when he'd registered the tightness of her incredible body, her startled gasp, and concluded it must have been a while since she had been with a man. Now he knew the truth: she had been a virgin, and his mouth twisted in a grimace of self-recrimination. He had treated her abominably. It wasn't surprising she was reluctant to marry him.

His heavy-lidded eyes swept over her lovely face and her scantily clad body. He was only a hand's reach away; he could feel her body heat, scent her unique fragrance, and the rigid control he had managed to maintain over his rampant libido finally snapped.

Charlie flinched as he closed the distance between them and rested a strong, lean hand on her shoulder. 'Charlotta,' he said. 'Please marry me.'

Her head told her to wait, step away. But her heart kept her still, the soft *please* echoing in her head. She felt the tremor in the hand that rested on her shoulder. He was so close that she could see the tell-tale darkening of his gorgeous eyes. And ultimately she said, 'Yes,' because she loved him and could not say no.

'Dio grazia.' Jake drew her into his arms, his mouth finding hers with unerring accuracy.

For Charlie it was like coming home, her body melting into his. Five long weeks of abstinence were echoed in the hunger of his mouth, the hot, unbridled passion that swept away all her doubts in a flood of excitement. She felt the hardness of his body against hers, and squirmed ecstatically against him. Jake was back and she wanted his hands on her breasts, her thighs, everywhere. She was starving for his touch, the taste of him, and she wrapped her arms around his neck, her fingers burrowing through the thick dark hair of his head, holding him to her.

He groaned against her mouth. '*Dio*, Charlotte, I have missed you, missed this.' His hands lifted and cupped her breasts, his fingers skimming over the cotton that covered her swelling flesh, and she moaned as his fingers plucked the sensitised peaks and a quick stab of arousal lanced from her nipples to her loins.

'Oh, Jake, I've missed you too, so much,' she sighed ecstatically as he nipped her bottom lip between his teeth, and kissed her again with a deep, hungry passion until she was mindless and shaking in his arms. 'I love you so much, love what you do to me,' she moaned, almost incoherently—but not quite.

'I know.' Jake smiled against her mouth. It was one of the things he adored about her, she was such a vocal lover, and slowly he slid his hand down her body. His long fingers curled beneath the hem of her shorts and he cupped her between her thighs, and she moaned his name again.

'Charlie, I need the keys to the safe…'

Jake's hand shot from between her thighs to grip her around the waist and hold her tight against him as he let fly with a string of Italian curses that would have made the devil blush.

'Oops! Not the best of timing, but I am glad to see you've kissed and made up.' Her manager's voice finally got through to Charlie's love-hazed mind.

'Jeff!' she squeaked, pushing against Jake's chest, her face the colour of a beetroot. 'Have you never heard of knocking?' She tried to squirm out of Jake's hold, dying inside with embarrassment.

'My sentiments exactly,' Jake said sardonically, looking at the other man over the top of Charlotte's head.

'Sorry.' Jeff grinned, looking not in the least sorry. 'So, Charlie, does this mean I can tell the staff wedding bells are on the cards, and finally put them out of their misery?' he queried, tongue in cheek.

Jake stilled, his brows drawing together in a puzzled frown, and then he suddenly grinned. 'Ah, now I understand the staff's attitude,' he said dryly.

'What attitude?' Charlie demanded. 'Was someone rude to you?'

'Not exactly, but let me guess. They all know you're pregnant, and they all know my name.'

'Well, I might have mentioned you in passing.' She had the grace to blush.

Jake laughed out loud, his arm tightening around her shoulders. 'As you appear to have been doing all the talking so far, at least allow me to make this announcement. As the man concerned, it is only fair,' he added mockingly.

Charlie stayed dumb.

'Jeff, isn't it? I believe we met earlier. As you have seen for yourself, Charlotte and I can't keep our hands off each other, and so, yes, we are getting married, just as soon as it can be arranged. Feel free to tell everyone. If you don't, I'm sure Charlotte will.'

'Certainly, Mr d'Amato.' Jeff laughed. 'Obviously you know our Charlie well. I'll just get the keys and leave.'

'So, Charlotte, it is done. We are to marry—no going back.' He drew her into his arms again.

'I won't change my mind.' Never one to duck a challenge, she asked bluntly, 'Is it because I'm pregnant? Or do you really love me?'

'Yes, *cara*. I adore you.' And he kissed her.

They were married two weeks later in an outdoor ceremony in the grounds of the hotel. The wedding breakfast was over and the speeches done, and Charlie, with Jake's arm around her shoulder, was still in shock from the speed of it all.

'One more and that's it.' Diego Fortuna, Jake's best man, was a famous fashion photographer.

'I feel as though I should strike a pose or something,' Charlie murmured, slightly intimidated.

'The *something* being, let's get out of here. I want you to myself. And I don't want to waste any more of our wedding day, or more importantly wedding night, chatting to your friends—nice as they are,' Jake added, his dark eyes roaming over the exquisite vision in ivory silk at his side. His wife. He congratulated himself on having made the right decision. He had discovered, on being introduced to quite a few of her male friends, that she was a member of the local mountain rescue team. Not only was she beautiful, and very beddable and carrying his child, she was also brave, though the climbing would have to stop, he decided. He didn't believe in love, but he had no trouble accepting Charlotte's declarations of love. Life didn't get any better than this.

'You have a one-track mind.' Charlie chuckled, her blue eyes laughing up at him.

'Do you blame me? It has been seven weeks.'

'No, I can't wait either,' she said honestly. She had never felt more loved, more cherished in her life than when the registrar had said, 'You may kiss the bride,' and Jake had taken her in his arms, and kissed her with a tenderness that had brought tears to her eyes. But now she wanted more.

The day he had proposed had turned into a party at the hotel, and by accident or design Jeff and Dave had turned it into a stag night for Jake. Pressure of business had forced Jake to leave early the next morning. Even so, he had with Jeff and Dave's assistance organised everything long distance. The only thing Charlie had done was shop for her trousseau. She had bought lacy underwear and a few totally impractical flimsy nightgowns. She had limited herself to one cocktail dress with the prospect of a bulging tummy in mind, and, ever practical, for her wedding outfit she had chosen an exquisitely made designer suit.

A sophisticated column of ivory silk, the dress was strapless and revealed a hint of cleavage before skimming her still slender figure to end just on her knees. Apart from a posy of rosebuds, her only other adornment was a choker of pearls around her throat. Jake had flown in last night and given them to her over dinner at the hotel, but they had not spent the night together. Amy, the receptionist, had made sure of that, saying it was unlucky, and sharing Charlie's room herself, much to Jake's chagrin.

Diego, the best man, had arrived this morning, and Charlie had met him for a few moments before the ceremony. He and Jake had been room-mates at college and were old friends, and he was almost as handsome as Jake.

'Right, that's it,' Diego cried. 'I need a drink.'

Charlie flung her posy into the crowd, and Amy, her bridesmaid, caught it amid much laughter. A few moments later Amy stepped forward and handed Charlie her suit jacket and her purse. 'Enjoy your honeymoon and have a wonderful life.'

'Thanks.' Charlie grinned.

'Thanks,' Jake echoed. 'Pressure of work means the honeymoon is on hold for the moment, unfortunately, but the wedding night isn't. Though we won't even have that if the damn car doesn't show up. I need to have a word with Dave,' he muttered darkly. Pressing a swift kiss on Charlie's smiling lips, he added, 'Wait here, I'm going to find out what's happened.'

Charlie watched her new husband stroll purposefully towards the hapless Dave. If she knew Dave, he had probably hijacked the car and covered it with bottles and cans and cheesy comments. She heaved a sigh of pure delight. This was the happiest day of her life.

'Big sigh for a new bride,' Diego said, reappearing with a glass of champagne in his hand.

'A sigh of pure happiness,' Charlie answered, slanting Diego a brilliant smile before her gaze sought out her husband. He looked so devastatingly handsome in a tailored silver-grey three-piece suit and she watched as he gesticulated wildly with one hand towards the drive. He was so very Latin, and she loved him.

'Changing your name from Summerville to d'Amato obviously suits you,' Diego said and drained the champagne.

'Yes, it does,' Charlie murmured, not paying much attention. All her thoughts were with Jake and the night ahead.

'Are you any relation to the artist Robert Summerville?' Diego asked.

'Yes, he was my father. In fact he was responsible for my meeting Jake,' she offered, remembering the first time she had seen Jake in the art gallery.

'Ah! Now I see,' Diego exclaimed. 'You have known Jake for much longer than I thought. I did wonder when he said he was getting married in two weeks. He is not the type to act in haste. But you must have known Anna when she lived with your father. You met Jake through her—or at her funeral, perhaps?' He shook his dark head. 'Her death so soon after your father's demise was such a tragedy.'

Charlie's brow furrowed as the full import of Diego's words sank in. Suddenly the nude painting Jake had bought when she met him loomed large in her mind. With it came the conviction she now had a name for her father's ex-lover—Anna—and if Diego was to be believed, she had been a close personal friend of Jake. But why hadn't Jake said anything?

Feeling a sudden chill that had nothing to do with the sunny weather, she slipped on the short jacket that matched her dress. 'You mean Anna with the beautiful long dark hair, almost to her thighs?' she queried softly, describing the woman in the portrait.

'That's her. So you did know her. It was a sad business all around, no? But what am I thinking of?' Diego grinned. 'Forgive me. Today is not a day for recalling past losses. Life is for celebrating.' He drained his brandy glass. 'Jake is a very lucky guy to have found you. I wish I had seen you first,' he added with a teasing, slightly inebriated glint in his eyes.

'You're a charmer.' Charlie smiled, but with difficulty. Diego had aroused a suspicion in her mind. There was a mystery here she did not understand. But he was right: this was not a day for recalling the past, but for looking forward to the future. Jake loved her, Jake had married her, and nothing was going to spoil her day.

'I was always the charmer,' Diego asserted, sliding an arm around her waist. 'And Jake was always the worker. But he did have his moments. Mostly with engines, rather than women,' he added drolly. 'Though he did once take a girl out on a powerboat he built, and it sank. Needless to say, she never spoke to him again.'

Twenty feet away Dave listened to Jake's tirade before slapping him on the back. 'Relax, Jake, the car will be here in five minutes. I understand you intend keeping our lovely Charlie in Italy? I hope you realise you're a very lucky man. She's an all-or-nothing kind of woman, so you'd better take very good care of her. We're all going to miss her at International Rapid Rescue. But I've told Charlie we'll be looking forward to seeing her back after she has the baby.'

'You…what?' Jake's black brows arched in amazement, and in the next few minutes he discovered he did not know his wife at all. That Charlotte would willingly risk her life in search and rescue all over the world appalled him. His head reared back, his eyes searching for her across the heads of the guests, and narrowed angrily when he saw she was talking to Diego, and the devil had his arm around her.

'Forget about Charlotte ever working again, Dave. I have other plans for her,' he threw over his shoulder as he made a beeline for her.

'What is this, a mutual admiration society? Get your arm off my wife, Diego.'

'Spoilsport.' Charlie grinned. 'Diego was just telling me about your college exploits.'

'Was he indeed?' Jake put his own arm around Charlotte, drawing her close into his side. He said something in rapid-fire Italian to Diego, who responded equally quickly, then turned a grin of pure devilment on Charlie.

'I am sorry you have to leave so soon, Charlotte. I feel I was just getting to know you, but I understand Jake's haste.' Taking a card from his pocket, he gave it to Charlie. 'This is my number. If you ever get tired of this jealous bozo, give me a call.'

'*Basta*, Diego, and stop trying to pick up my wife on our wedding day,' Jake growled.

'As if I would.' Diego winked at Charlie. 'Though I have tried with the lovely Amy—unfortunately she's already taken. But I now have my eye on a rather attractive barmaid.' Waving his empty glass, he said, 'Wish me luck,' and headed for the bar.

'Diego is fun. I like him.'

Moving her supple body in front of him, Jake looked down into her luminous sapphire eyes. 'Not too much, I trust; you're my wife now.' With his free hand he cradled the back of her head and kissed her passionately.

A scarlet-faced Charlie heard the cheers of the guests, and Dave's yell that the wedding car had arrived, in something of a daze. Jake took an exaggerated bow, and she had to laugh as he swung her into his arms and carried her to the waiting vehicle.

'Oh, my God!' she squealed. She had been right about the cans, bottles and slightly dubious graffiti scrolled all over the white limousine. But Jake, not in the least fazed, lowered her into the back seat and quickly followed her.

'Now I see why the car was delayed.' He chuckled and with a single finger he outlined her softly parted lips. 'But you, my darling wife, are worth any wait. You're so beautiful, you make me ache.' And his mouth took hers in a kiss of such wondrous promise and passion she knew that whatever the future held for them she would always love Jake—her husband.

CHAPTER EIGHT

A LIMOUSINE met them at Genoa airport and, tucked under Jake's arm, Charlie gazed out of the window as the car cruised along a winding road by the sea and into the hills, stopping at a massive pair of iron gates, complete with gate-house. A security guard opened the gates and the car sped up a mile-long drive to what to Charlie looked like a mansion.

Jake helped her out of the car and she looked up in awe. The house was magnificent. Of surprisingly modern design, it was mostly constructed in glass and steel. It was situated a few miles from Genoa, with the Dolomites as a backdrop, and a spectacular view of the Mediterranean to the front.

'Your new home, Signora d'Amato. Do you like it?'

'It's spectacular.' Laughing, Jake swept her up in his arms and carried her through the massive double doors. 'Oh, my God, a glass staircase! It's fantastic,' Charlie exclaimed, and then she realised a reception committee of two were waiting in the enormous hall.

Lowering her to her feet, Jake introduced her to Marta, a pretty, dark-haired lady, and Charlie blushed as she shook her hand, remembering her crazy call. Then she was introduced to an adorable little boy, Marta's son Aldo, and to Charlie's delight he spoke to her in good schoolboy English. Marta's husband Tomas joined them: he was the chauffeur, and a bottle of champagne was produced and a toast drunk. Then Tomas and his family departed to their cottage in the grounds with smiles and grins, and Jake closed and locked the door behind them.

Charlie looked around. The furniture was an eclectic mix of traditional and modern but it was the paintings that caught her attention. She recognised a Matisse and two Monets.

'At last we are alone.' Jake swept her up in his arms and carried her up the stairs. Her shoes fell off and she tightened her grip around his neck with a startled, 'Oh!'

'One less item to remove.' Jake gave her a wicked grin and they both burst out laughing as he walked into the master bedroom.

With less than his usual grace, he stumbled over her suitcases already deposited in the bedroom. 'Don't you dare drop me,' Charlie commanded, still laughing.

'Never,' Jake responded with an abashed grin. Their eyes met and the laughter stopped.

Slowly he lowered her to her feet, and her eyes widened fractionally as he touched a gentle finger to her lips and traced the upper outline, and then the lower curve. Incredibly she suddenly felt nervous. She had slept with Jake countless times, but this time was different.

Jake's eyes didn't leave hers as he stepped back and shrugged off his jacket and tie. Then, with slow, deliberate movements, he removed the rest of his clothes until he was standing before her, tall and broad-shouldered with bronzed skin sheathing hard-backed muscle and sinew and wearing only white silk briefs that did little to hide his arousal. Warm colour tinged her cheeks, and for a long moment she simply stared, the sexual tension simmering between them.

'No need to be nervous, Charlotte,' Jake said, accurately reading her mind, and closed the distance between them. 'Have I told you today you look beautiful, *cara*?' he asked softly as he lowered his head down to hers.

Warmth flooded her body and became a pulsing heat as he slid her jacket from her shoulders, and a moan sounded in her throat at the touch of his mouth on her own.

His hands skimmed her breasts, and down her thighs, and in one fluid movement the raw silk dress slid down to pool at her feet leaving her naked except for delicate white lace French panties.

Jake stepped back, the better to appreciate her lush shapely body tantalisingly enhanced by the pearl choker and the seductively cut lace panties. Her breasts were fuller, her stomach where his child lay still flat.

'I feel as if I have waited a lifetime to see you like this.'

It was incomprehensible, but Charlie, who had the confidence to do anything, was suddenly plagued by self-doubt as Jake's dark, obsessive gaze roamed intently over her. He was so perfect, tall and golden, and she wanted to be perfect for him, but she was pregnant and it was over seven weeks since they had been together. Her breasts were fuller, not so firm, and Jake was used to perfection: his house, his art.

Her eyes flicked past him in a brief panicky movement and she saw the picture on the wall behind him. It was a Gauguin, an island woman with long black hair, and it reminded her of another painting and Diego's comment about Anna.

Jake's hands reached for her and settled on her waist.

'Who was Anna?' She murmured the thought even as her eyes were drawn back to meet smouldering black and the uninhibited desire, the raw hunger she saw there ignited a fire deep in her belly.

But as she swayed towards him his head reared back, his fingers digging into her waist almost to the point of pain in a knee-jerk re-action to her question. 'Where the hell did that come from?' he ground out harshly.

'It was nothing,' she said quickly. 'I caught sight of the painting on the wall and it reminded me of the painting you bought and something Diego said today.'

Jake's face hardened, but his hands eased slightly on her waist. 'Diego has a big mouth. Whatever he said, forget it, and drop the sub-ject.'

If the command had not been so curtly delivered Charlie might have done so, but his strange attitude made her all the more determined to get to the bottom of the mystery.

Before she could lose her nerve she said, 'Diego thought you and I might have met earlier, because she was my father's lover and also a friend of yours. He actually thought Anna might have introduced us.' Drawing in a shaky breath, she asked the question she had wanted to avoid. 'Was she an ex-lover of yours?'

'*Dio*, no.' Jake was angry, ridiculously angry, and he had no right to be. Her question was ill-timed, but perfectly valid. Unfortunately, the subject of Anna aroused conflicting emotions inside him: the loyalty he owed to the Lasios, the guilt he could not quite dismiss, and the frustration he felt that his wife of a few hours was looking at him with puzzled rather than passion-filled eyes.

Flattening her hands on his shoulders, she tilted back her head. 'Then why won't you tell me who she was?'

'You know who she was,' he said with a harsh laugh that was no laugh at all. 'She was the lover of your lecherous father, and over twenty years his junior. Now let's forget her, and concentrate on us.' He pulled her hard against him. 'This is our wedding night, and arguing with you was not what I had in mind.'

He was being evasive, but he was also right. A few seconds of feminine insecurity and she had ruined the mood. Why hadn't she kept her mouth shut? Because she was curious about the mysterious Anna of the portrait. She sighed, answering her own question.

'I'd like to think that was a sigh for me, for sex,' Jake said dryly. 'But I rather think it is frustration of another sort: your insatiable curiosity about a certain painting.'

He had read her mind and she flushed a little, but there was no point in denying it.

He shrugged his broad shoulders, his austerely handsome face suddenly devoid of all expression. 'You want the truth? Why not? According to all the marriage pundits, it's the way to go for a good marriage and so far ours appears to be going nowhere fast.' His voice was sardonic. 'Anna was my foster-sister, and I loved her. I was there when she was born, I watched her grow into a beautiful young woman, and I saw her destroyed by your father. She imagined herself in love with him and for two years she thought he was going to marry her.'

Charlie paled as the full import of his words sank in. The relief she had felt that Anna had never been Jake's lover vanished as she realised the truth was much worse. An ex-lover could be forgotten, but a sister never.

When she had met Jake he'd told her the painting was the only one he wanted. Not surprising if, as Diego had said, Anna had died recently. She remembered the look in the girl's eyes. And she remembered the glazed look in Jake's when he'd looked at it. How he must have hated to see her exposed like that…

A host of moments with Jake spun in the whirlpool of her mind, and began to assume a different meaning. Their first night together. She recalled his coldness after they had made love, his questioning her as to what she thought about an older man taking a young woman as a lover. Naively she had thought he was referring to the twelve-year gap between them. Now she realised he must have been thinking of her father.

She caught her breath in shock. 'My God! You hated my father.' She stared at him in horror. 'I'm right, aren't I?'

'I never met him, but, yes, I hated him.' Jake slid a lean hand around her waist. 'But don't let it bother you.' His voice was almost mocking. 'The man is dead, as is Anna. And you are my wife.' His other hand stroked down her throat and deftly unfastened the choker so it fell unheeded to the floor before trailing lower to cup her breast, a thumb testing the hardening peak. 'And we have wasted enough time already.'

'No.' She tried to deny him, but her treacherous flesh was already craving more. 'Let go of me,' she said jaggedly in an atmosphere suddenly raw with sexual tension. 'We need to talk.'

'What you need is very evident.' His dark eyes slanted down to her naked breast, where the rigid tip was a real give-away, then back to her face. His mouth touched hers, very lightly. 'And it certainly isn't talk. It is me, *cara*.'

The arrogance of his comment and the truth of it mortified her and inflamed her temper at one and the same time. He admitted he hated her father and in the next breath expected her to fall into his arms. His conceit was monumental, and, twisting out of his hold, she took a hasty step back and crossed her arms defensively over her aching breasts.

She was an intelligent woman, and with hindsight suddenly a lot of little things he had said made sense. While she had been driven by an all-consuming desire, even love, for Jake straight into his bed, she was now forced to question what had been his real motivation. The day they had gone to the museum, he had joked about his motivation, and the answer, she saw now, had been enigmatic.

Closing her eyes for a moment, she slowly fought to achieve a semblance of self-control, then, opening them again, she flicked a glance at his hard, handsome face.

'No, Jake, what I need from you is the truth,' she said, proud of her ability to control the tremor in her voice, even though inside she was shaking like a leaf. 'Why did you ask Ted to introduce you to me at the gallery? Surely if you hated my father so much I must have been the last person you would want to know?' Her mouth was dry as she waited for his response.

'I was curious to see what kind of daughter a man who had so little respect for women had produced. But what does it matter now?' He shrugged. 'We are married and have the future to look forward to.'

She saw the familiar shuttered look in his eyes that protected his deepest thoughts, and knew he was not telling her the whole truth. But she was achingly aware of how much she loved him. Her wedding night was fast turning into a nightmare, not what she wanted at all. Jake was right, none of it mattered any more, and she unfolded her arms and took a tentative step towards him.

'I am sorry about your sister, Jake.' She swallowed hard. The words were inadequate, she knew. 'No one knows better than me what a womanising rogue my father was. And if Anna loved him it must have been terrible for her when he died. I know how I felt, and I know the hurt you must have felt when Anna died. What can I say?'

Slowly his eyes drifted over her—assessing eyes that did not betray a flicker of warmth. Not the reaction she had expected for her sympathy. 'Nothing, nothing at all,' he finally drawled. His arm once more slipped around her waist, and with his free hand he tilted her head back. 'It has already been said.' And the sizzling scorn in the black eyes that clashed with hers sent a shiver of fear snaking down her spine. 'Your father sent Anna away and we both know why. So you can drop the mock sympathy.' His mouth twisted in a hard, humourless smile. 'You refused to meet her.'

For a split second Charlie was convinced she had heard wrong. But his dark eyes held contempt and the immobility of his hard features told her she had not.

'I refused to meet her?' she parroted. When she had visited her dad for a couple of weeks three months before his death, he had told her he was between lovers. Not that she'd believed him; it had been his standard response for years in his misguided attempt to protect Charlie from his women. But Jake had a different view. Why, she had no idea.

'Anna told me everything. Your father sent her away because his *bitch of a daughter* insisted upon it. Apparently the girl was arriving for a holiday and she was so selfish she refused to share her father with his lover. Brave of you to admit it, I suppose,' Jake allowed dryly.

'I can't believe what you're saying!' Charlie shook her head free of his controlling fingers, her mind sifting the information Jake had given her with lightning speed. The full horror of what he implied chilled her to the bone, the conclusion unmistakable. The relationship between her father and Anna was immaterial. Jake, her lover, her husband, thought she was a selfish bitch.

'No,' she murmured, briefly closing her eyes, Jake could not possibly believe that of her. She opened them again; her stunned gaze met his. 'I loved my father, but—' She was going to explain it was her father who never allowed her to meet his lovers, not the other way around.

'But, as they say, the rest is history,' Jake cut in mockingly. 'Your father died—if he hadn't I would have destroyed him myself—and Anna crashed her car into a tree a few months later and followed him to the grave. But on the upside you made a lot of money, so it's not all doom and gloom. Now forget it. The past is past. It is the present that concerns me.'

The past shapes the future. Charlie had read that somewhere, and Jake's throwaway comments that he would have destroyed her father given the chance, and about the money he thought she'd made by his death, made her sick to her stomach. But she had to hear the truth from his mouth, however much it hurt. She had been blinded by love for far too long.

She tried to pull free of him, but he tightened his arm around her waist and she refused to demean herself by struggling. 'Given you thought I was not just a selfish bitch, but greedy as well…' her voice was flat and toneless, and she wondered how it was possible for her skin to burn at the contact with his while an icy chill built up inside her '…tell me again why you asked Ted to introduce us. The truth, this time.'

The muscles in his jaw tightened for an instant, and then his chiselled features relaxed, and his dark eyes gleamed with a hint of self-deprecatory humour as they meshed with hers. 'Truthfully? Because Anna had given me the impression Summerville's daughter was a child. When Ted told me you were a businesswoman who had sanctioned the exhibition, I wanted to meet you. What I could forgive in a child, I could not forgive in an adult, and I admit revenge did cross my mind. Poetic justice, if you like. But to be honest, I took one look at you and wanted you, *cara*. Still do.'

Revenge was such an ugly word, and such an ugly emotion, and at first Charlie did not want to believe what she was hearing. But as it sank in she was horrified at his colossal confidence, his despicable arrogance—that he would assume she was such a pushover that she would accept such an explanation and continue as though nothing had happened. She swallowed hard. 'Why did you ask me to marry you?' She had to know the worst.

'You are carrying my child, Charlotte.' His free hand slipped to her stomach and rested there.

Tears of anger and pain stung her eyes, and she fought them back, achingly aware of his strong, near-naked body touching her own from chest to thigh, but also finally aware—on her wedding night, of all nights—that Jake didn't love her, never had, and probably never would.

She wanted to scream and yell her pain to the world as her heart shattered into a million pieces. But she didn't. Instead the chill inside her grew until a blessed numbness froze the pain and she said, in a voice that seemed to come from a long way off, 'And to think when you proposed, I asked you if you loved me, and you lied and said yes.'

'As I remember you asked if I was marrying you because you were pregnant or because I loved you, and I answered yes, I adored you.' His unreadable eyes swept her carefully controlled features, a smile as insincere as any she had seen curving his beautiful mouth. 'How you interpreted my response was up to you.'

'A question of semantics,' she mocked hollowly, and dragged her gaze from his. The revelations this evening had cut her to the bone. But she could not betray her weakness. She had to be strong, not just for herself but also for her child. With a proud tilt of her head she looked at him coldly, her voice displaying no trace of emotion as she said, 'Be honest, Jake, you don't love me. All I ever was to you was a body to enjoy while you fed your sick need for revenge, but unfortunately I got pregnant.'

'You're wrong. I no longer have any need for revenge, and as for enjoying your body…' His dark eyes gleamed with sardonic humour. 'So far I am not having much luck, but that is about to change.'

His dark head bent and she saw it in his eyes, felt it in the tightening grip of his hands, and she knew he was going to kiss her. Belatedly Charlie lifted her own hands and shoved against his chest. 'No.' She struggled frantically, her hands curling into fists, and she punched him on the chest—anywhere she could reach. 'No, no!' she cried.

His mouth silenced hers and the possessive passion of his kiss and the sudden heated response that arced through her completely shamed her. Charlie tore her mouth from his and struck out wildly, but with his superior height and strength he simply swept her up in his arms, and deposited her surprisingly gently on the bed.

Lashing out with her feet, Charlie scrambled up into a sitting position. 'Don't you touch me, don't you dare,' she yelled. 'And you can take your damn ring!' she cried, twisting desperately at the wedding band on her finger.

Rage tore through Jake and, leaning over her, he grasped her hands in one of his before she could remove the ring from her finger. 'Leave it, Charlotte!' he roared. And as he saw the hurt and fury in her eyes he froze.

What the hell was he doing? Drawing a deep, shuddering breath, he let go of her hands and straightened up. He could not argue with her. She was upset, and she was pregnant.

Frustration riding him, he stared down at her, his eyes raking over her body: the high, full breasts, the narrow waist and the gentle rounded curves of her hips; the transparent scrap of lace she was wearing doing little to hide the shadow of her femininity... No, he could not go there. Abruptly he raised his eyes to her face. She was looking at him as if he had developed two horns and a tail, and it was his own damned fault. Whichever marriage expert had recommended absolute truth needed their head read. If he had not been so out of his mind with sexual hunger for Charlotte, he might have had the sense to keep his mouth shut.

But he wouldn't be in this unenviable position if someone else had kept his mouth shut, he thought bitterly, silently cursing Diego for mentioning Anna and ruining his wedding night. He had burned the damned painting weeks ago. He didn't care about revenge; he didn't care about anything except Charlotte, he realised with shock. His stunned gaze roved over her flushed face, he saw the defiance in her gorgeous eyes, and felt a sharp pang of regret for the loss of her unfeigned adoration. And a frustrated fury he could barely control.

'The only thing I want to leave is you.' Charlotte slotted the words into the lengthening silence. Jake took a step closer. His dark eyes narrowed to angry slits, and she drew in a stunned, slightly unsteady breath.

'You are not going anywhere.' His face was a taut mask of rigidly controlled rage. 'But I will leave.' For one heart-stopping moment she thought he meant for good. 'We will talk about this in the morning.' Dipping down, he retrieved something from the floor and flung it at her. 'When hopefully you remember why you wore that today, and grow up.' And spinning on his heel, he left, slamming the door behind him.

The sound echoed in the sudden silence of the room as Charlie fingered the crumpled wedding dress he had thrown at her, the events of the evening racing through her tormented mind. This was her wedding night. How had it gone so terribly wrong? Because she had finally chipped through Jake's—her husband's—monumental control and discovered the truth, and it was not the love she had hoped and dreamed of.

White-knuckled, she gripped the gown and began to shiver. Acting on autopilot, she slipped off the bed. She found her suitcase and withdrew a blue satin nightgown, then shoved her wedding dress inside and shut the case. She slid the blue satin over her head. It wasn't very warm, but then she had not bought it with warmth in mind. She blinked and blinked again as she walked back to the bed, and lay back down, pulling the sheet up over her shaking body. Then, and only then, she buried her head in a pillow and surrendered to the agony and despair that tore at her very soul. Finally when there were no more tears left, only dry racking sobs, and her stomach ached with the pain, she realised she had to stop—if not for herself, for the sake of the baby.

She didn't know what she was going to do. All she did know was the happy, laughing bride of a few hours ago was no more. Jake had seen to that. 'Damn Jake—damn him to hell,' she muttered under her breath as hurt and anger rose to the fore. Who the hell did he think he was? What right had he to sit in judgement of her or her father's morals when he had the morals of an alley cat by all accounts?

Charlie tossed restlessly on the bed. She had to be strong. Already she was coming to terms with the revelations this evening had brought, and given time she would work out the best plan of action. She was an independent woman, or had been before she had met Jake and let love cloud her judgement—but no more, and no more tears. She rubbed her eyes with the sheet. And if Jake thought she was going to sit around playing the grateful little wife and mother, Jake was in for a rude awakening.

With his name lingering on her lips she fell into an exhausted sleep, unaware that her husband had returned and was staring down at her. He saw the tears that leaked from under her pale lids as she slept, and sorrow dampened his eyes as he quietly turned and left.

CHAPTER NINE

'GOOD, you're awake.'

Charlie shot up in bed, her gaze winging to the door, her eyes widening in shock as Jake, barefoot and wearing a maroon silk robe, entered the room. In his hands was a tray set with breakfast with a vase containing a single red rose as a centrepiece. 'Not quite the conventional honeymoon breakfast of champagne, due to your condition. But I have made you tea and scrambled eggs on toast.' He smiled, approaching the bed.

Jake looked so pleased with himself, Charlie had to fight back a reciprocal smile and consequently she said more harshly than she intended, 'You needn't have bothered.'

'Hostilities resumed, I see,' Jake mocked, his eyes darkening, a muscle tightening in his jaw as he placed the tray down on the bedside table.

For a fleeting moment she regretted ignoring what was obviously an olive branch from Jake, but only for a moment. The hurt had gone too deep for Charlie to forgive or forget. 'I'm pregnant, not an invalid. I could have made my own breakfast.'

'You don't need to; that's Marta's job. But I gave her the day off for some reason that escapes me now,' he said sardonically. He filled a cup with tea and handed it to her and, careful to avoid touching his hand, she took it.

'Thank you,' she murmured, slanting a glance at his handsome face.

A cynical light gleamed in the dark eyes that met hers. '*Prego.* Eat, enjoy, and we will talk.'

'I don't see we have much to talk about. You said it all last night.' She drank the tea, and replaced the cup on the tray. She didn't want to talk; she didn't want to look at him. Charlie felt as though a veil had been torn from her eyes last night and for the first time since she had met Jake she had seen him in his true colours. He was a ruthless, hard-hearted bastard who hit back at anyone who crossed him, as he perceived her father had—and her as well.

'Last night I said too damn much.' Jake snorted disgustedly. 'But the past is dead and buried with your father and Anna. Surely you can see that?' he asked seriously. 'We were married yesterday. Forget last night and let us start again.' Sitting down on the side of the bed, he covered her hand where it lay on the coverlet with his much larger one.

The sensual warmth of his touch triggered an immediate response in Charlie that filled her with dismay and a rising anger. Hastily she jerked her hand away, and, taking a deep calming breath, she raised her head. Blue eyes clashed with black and for a moment she was stunned by the tenderness in Jake's expression—but then, he was a great deceiver, she reminded herself.

'You might find it convenient to forget last night, but I never will. I must have been stark raving mad to marry you. You are a devious, rotten liar.' She had behaved like the world's biggest fool, and it hurt, it hurt like hell to know she had fallen so completely for Jake while he had a totally different agenda. But no way was she compounding her folly by continuing with this sham. 'And I want out of this fiasco of a marriage.' The smile left his handsome face and if she hadn't known him better she would have thought he was in pain, but then his dark brown eyes narrowed to angry slits and the air between them was suddenly electric with tension.

'Don't be ridiculous, Charlotte. I—'

She cut him off sharply. 'I'm not being ridiculous, just stating a fact. I want out.'

Nobody called Jake a liar and got away with it, not even Charlotte. 'Never. You are my wife,' he sliced back, his gaze roaming over her beautiful but mutinous face and lower to where the creamy mounds of her breast were temptingly revealed by the slip of blue satin that passed as a nightgown. Jake's control was stretched to the limit. He felt bad about throwing the dress at her last night, but it had been either that or throwing himself on her. He had had such high hopes this morning when he had made breakfast that she would put the unpleasantness of last night behind her and act like a reasonable adult. But if anything she was more determined to defy him than ever, while he was getting more frustrated by the second, as the ache in his groin reminded him. 'You will stay in my home,' he commanded in a dangerously quiet voice. 'And in my bed. Understand?'

Charlie shivered, her flesh chilled at the deadly certainty with which he voiced his intentions. But she refused to be cowed. She had been a doormat for far too long.

'In your dreams. I'm out of here tomorrow.'

'No.' He shook his head.

Succinct and clearly unmovable. She realised it had not been the most sensible time to tell him when she was still in bed. He was staring at her, his chiselled features as hard as stone while a savage, sensual smile played around his mouth. She tore her gaze from his, but a strong hand cupped her chin and turned her back to face him. Her pulse beat a frantic rhythm through her whole body at his touch, and she was horrified at her own weakness.

'I am not staying here with you. Not now.'

His smile was softly derisive. 'You have no choice in the matter. The security around here is superb. You don't leave without my say-so.'

'You can't force me to stay here. You wouldn't dare,' Charlie flung back at him, but she saw the implacable gleam in his dark eyes and knew he would dare anything to get what he wanted.

'I won't have to. I know you, Charlotte. You want the best for our child and you know that is both parents living together in harmony.' Sliding his hand around the nape of her neck, he urged her head forward, and brushed his lips against her cheek. 'I also know you are too proud to return to England and admit failure,' he added and, dipping his head, captured her mouth in a deeply provocative kiss.

In direct opposition to her will, a slow fire began to course though her veins, bringing every nerve in her body to tingling life. The seductive pressure of his mouth and her own heated response was totally humiliating and yet when he broke the kiss she felt bereft. Then she noticed where his gaze had fixed and, grasping the sheet, she raised it up over her chest, suddenly aware of the brevity of the nightgown she had donned unthinkingly last night.

The dark eyes narrowed knowingly on her flushed face. 'It is allowable, Charlotte,' he mocked. 'You're my wife, the soon-to-be mother of my child. Concentrate on that and we will get along fine.'

Charlie saw the arrogance, the supreme masculine confidence in his gaze and her eyes closed against the pain she felt deep inside. She wanted to cry, but her pride would not let her, and pride was all she had left. She opened her eyes. 'Given that according to you I am trapped in this place, it would seem I don't have much of a choice,' she said scathingly. 'What do you intend to do, lock me up?'

Jake's expression changed to one of frustrated fury. '*Dio*, no! But the way you are behaving could drive a man to it,' he snarled. 'Damn it to hell, Charlotte. How do you expect me to react when you declare you want to end our marriage before it has even begun? Over a damned painting—and not a very good one at that!' he added with biting sarcasm.

'A painting you lied to me about the night we met,' she said bitterly. 'You said you wanted it for an investment, dead artist and all that. I believed you because you looked that hard-headed. But I should have guessed you had a deeper purpose, when I saw the mesmerised way you looked at it. I should have left.'

Jake stared at her, and remained silent for what seemed an age. His voice when he finally spoke was menacingly soft. 'Not much of a lie. For any other purchaser it could be the truth. As for being mesmerised—I blanked it out because it felt incestuous to see it. I only looked at it because it was expected of me, as I had just bought the damn thing. I bought it to destroy it before Anna's parents discovered its existence. They have suffered enough pain losing their daughter, without the added pain of seeing her naked body displayed to the world. And you, Charlotte, might have thought of that before you blithely exposed your father's private collection to the public without having the decency to ask those concerned, simply to make money.'

Charlie found it difficult to swallow the lump that rose in her throat at his reason for buying the painting. It had been a noble gesture to prevent the people he cared about being hurt. But his last comment had confirmed yet again what she already knew: he did see her as a selfish, greedy bitch. Not a good basis for marriage.

Suddenly her pain gave way to angry resentment. She could explain the money was for charity, but the arrogant swine did not deserve to know. Jake was so damned sure of himself—so confident he was right about everything. Not two minutes ago he had been telling her he knew her well. What a joke! 'You assume I am a money-grubber, but you don't really know me at all,' she said bitterly. He could think what the hell he liked for all she cared.

Jake shook his head in disgust at himself. His image of Charlotte as a calculating woman who had been lucky enough to inherit a business and exploited her father's inheritance had mellowed in the two weeks they had spent together. Being brutally honest, he would probably have seen the art exhibition as a wise business decision, if it hadn't contained the picture of Anna. And Charlotte's refusal of a designer wardrobe and her delight in a soft toy, plus Dave's revelation about her rescue work, had blasted any doubts he had had into oblivion.

'Maybe I don't, but I want to. Which is why we need to talk,' he said quietly, his long, lean fingers tightening the belt of his robe around his waist. Watching him, Charlie had the oddest notion he was nervous. Glancing at his face, her blue eyes met guarded black, and, intrigued, she bit back the denial that hovered on her lips.

'My fault, if you could call it that, was in not revealing the intimate details of people I cared about when we met. And let's be honest, you are as guilty of concealing aspects of your life as I. It took a wedding guest to tell me you were in the mountain rescue team, and Dave's revelation that you worked for him with the International Rapid Rescue Team was a hell of a shock.'

'The subject never came up,' Charlie said defensively, watching him with wary eyes, not sure where he was leading.

'Perhaps we have both been less than open with each other, Charlotte. But as of now it has to stop—along, I might add, with any notion in that crazy head of yours that you will ever risk your life and limb with a rescue team of any kind again.' His eyes were narrowed intently on her face as he paused for a moment. 'We owe it to our unborn child to try and make this marriage a success, and with that in mind the first rule is we forget about the past, and move on from here. We have a lot going for us. We are great in bed together—you can't deny the chemistry is there—and I am a wealthy man. I can provide you with everything you need. Neither you nor our child will ever want for anything. What more could a wife want?' he demanded, and had the bare-faced nerve to smile at her.

Love, she thought, but could not say it, as her throat ached with the effort to hold back the tears that threatened for her lost dreams. 'Nothing, you're right,' she agreed, not believing him for a second. His concept of marriage horrified her. It was nothing more than a business deal: he paid the money and got the wife and child. But what were her options?

She couldn't think and the pressure of trying to retain her composure instead of bawling her eyes out stopped her from arguing with him. She lifted a hand and rubbed her temple in an attempt to ease the dull throbbing there.

'Here, let me do that.' Jake reached out and cupped her head in his hands.

For a moment Charlie stiffened, but only for a moment as his thumbs gently massaged her temples, soothing and unthreatening. Charlie's eyelids drifted shut in helpless response to the incredible sensitivity of his touch. The pressure in her temple eased and she breathed in deeply and sighed.

'Better?' Jake asked.

'Much,' she murmured, slowly opening her eyes. His face was only inches from her own, and the hands that had been holding her head dropped to her shoulders as his wide, sensual mouth closed over hers. Taking advantage of her open-mouthed surprise, he slid his tongue between her parted lips.

She raised her hands to push him away, but they met with the hard, hot wall of his chest and lingered as he deepened the kiss with a skilful, persuasive expertise. Her passionate re-sponse was humiliating but undeniable, and when his mouth moved from her lips to suck the sensitive hollow at the base of her throat, a low moan escaped her.

'I want you,' Jake rasped. His dark eyes, black with barely controlled desire, seared into hers as his hands on her shoulders eased her back against the pillows, his body following her down. 'You're mine, Charlotte. Forget the rest and let our marriage start here.'

The intensity of his gaze thrilled even as it threatened her, and she willed herself not to respond, but it was hopeless. The husky sound of his voice alone seduced her even as his sensual mouth claimed hers once more. His teeth nipped at her lower lip, and then soothed with a lick of his tongue, before probing the soft inner tissue of her mouth.

A low moan escaped her as he broke the kiss and reared up over her. Shrugging off his robe, Jake grasped the straps of blue satin at her shoulders and stripped the nightgown from her. His hot dark eyes studied her naked body with hungry pleasure. 'You are so beautiful.' His gaze lingered on her full breasts before lifting to her flushed face.

Charlie felt her whole body blush, heat racing through her. Her eyes skated helplessly over his handsome face, noting the sensuous curve to his full lips, and on down to the broad expanse of his muscular chest, the curling black body hair, down past his navel, and back to his face. She was totally mesmerised by the sheer masculine perfection of him, as she had always been.

Jake lifted one long finger and, with a feather-light touch, traced the curve of her cheek, her lips, her throat, and lower to her breast. 'Exquisite,' he said huskily. 'I want to taste you.'

His dark head lowered, his firm lips following the trail his finger had taken, lingering on her lips, more tempting than demanding, and then lower, to draw the aching peak of her breast into the heat of his mouth.

Her slender body arched involuntarily to the source of its pleasure, even as his fingers slid tantalisingly between her thighs. The musky male scent of him, his exquisite touch, had ignited a fire inside her only his full possession could douse.

'*Dio*, I need you, Charlotte,' he groaned, his sensuous mouth claiming hers once more. She felt it in the hunger of his kiss, and the pressure of his fiercely aroused flesh against her thigh.

The fact he had said *need* rather than *want* somehow inflamed her senses to fever pitch. Her fingers tangled in the silken hair of his head as he broke the kiss to trail a tongue of flame down her throat and lave the rigid peaks of her breast with tongue and teeth. And all the while his hands continued to caress her quivering flesh.

'You want me, Charlotte.' His dark head lifted from her breast, his glittering gaze seeking hers. 'And, *Dio*, I want you. I always have,' he groaned.

He was right. There was no point in denial. She loved him and her body ached for his, while he only lusted after hers, she knew. But she no longer cared as, driven by an unstoppable passion, she pressed her mouth to his throat. She bit his satin-smooth skin, felt his body tighten, and exulted in his husky groan. Her hands roamed feverishly over his powerful muscled body. She caressed and teased with mouth and teeth, using all the skills he had taught her, and he returned the favour. Pacing her pleasure with his own, he led her with a skilful, erotic ease to the very brink of ecstasy over and over again, until she almost wept from the sheer wonder of it.

He raised himself away from her, his night-black eyes molten with desire burning down into hers as he lifted her hips and surged into her, and the cry that rose in her throat was stilled as his mouth closed over hers.

She felt the quivering tension in his great frame as he thrust deeper and faster, her body instinctively picking up his rhythm. Her fingers dug into his bronzed skin and she was conscious only of Jake and the incredible joy of his possession, until the pleasure was almost too exquisite to bear. The fusion of their two bodies was mystical in its intensity, and she bit her lip to stop from screaming his name even as her body convulsed in a shattering climax that met and absorbed Jake's pulsating release.

His head fell to her shoulder, his harsh groan of masculine satisfaction echoing in her ears. She felt the heavy pounding of his heart against her own, their sweat-slicked bodies still shuddering in the aftershock of passion. She let her hands rove possessively over his damp skin, knowing that Jake had proved once again on a physical level they were in perfect accord.

Had it ever been that profound before? she thought dazedly. Her own aggression had sparked a fierce reaction in Jake, raw in its intensity, but with a phenomenal control he had excited her almost to the edge of oblivion and the final incredible climax had been the deepest, most potent fulfilment of all.

Maybe their marriage could work after all…

'Now you are truly my wife, *mia amore*,' Jake said huskily, burying his face in her mass of hair. But his last words struck a jarring note in her mind.

'Don't call me that,' Charlotte said sharply.

'Why not? You are my wife.' Jake raised his head, his dark eyes smiling lazily down at her. 'I seem to remember we got married yesterday.'

She saw the amusement in his gaze and the sense of betrayal came flooding back. 'As if I could forget.' She turned her head away. It was not the *wife* she was objecting to, but the *mia amore—my love*. But she had no intention of telling him so. That he should use the term of endearment now, when he never had before, was like a knife to the heart. Their lovemaking had been so perfect, but remembering what he had revealed earlier made her want to weep.

She was not his love, never had been, and never would be. She meant no more to Jake than any of the other women who had shared his bed. Less! Because he had as good as admitted he thought she was a greedy bitch, and he had only taken her out to get revenge.

'Charlotte.' He lifted up on one elbow, and looked down at her, his dark eyes gleaming with gentle amusement. 'I know what is the matter. You never ate your breakfast.' He reached out and smoothed the tangled mass of blonde hair from her brow in a gentle gesture. 'My fault again. In your condition you need food at regular intervals.'

'And who made you a doctor?' Charlie sniped back, his tenderness more than she could bear right now. But his reaction stunned her.

'Oh, hell!' He glanced at his watch, the only thing he was wearing, and leapt off the bed. 'I have a meeting later this morning, but first you and I have an appointment with a doctor in exactly forty-five minutes. It won't take me ten minutes to get ready next door, and I'll make you a sandwich—you can eat it in the car, because allowing for travelling time, you only have thirty minutes to get ready.'

'You have some nerve!' He was standing there, unashamedly naked, ordering her around, and Charlie was incensed. 'I am not going anywhere with you.' Her blue eyes blazed defiance.

'Just because we had sex, it does not mean you can tell me what to do.'

'We did not *just* have sex, and we do not have time to argue yet again. And you are going to the doctor if I have to carry you there.'

A naked man should not be able to look arrogant and threatening, but somehow Jake managed it, Charlie thought helplessly. 'What on earth for? I'm fine,' she asked, curbing her temper.

Jake gave her a hard look, and lashed out, 'What do you think? To confirm the state of your pregnancy, of course. After all, that is why I married you.' He knew he was speaking in a moment of anger, but he had thought everything was back on track between them. Now, looking at Charlotte, he doubted it. 'You have twenty-five minutes,' he flung over his shoulder as he left the room.

He could not have spelt out more clearly why he had married her if he had carved it in stone. And with that knowledge Charlie's heart turned to ice in her breast.

Twenty minutes later, wearing a blue and white patterned chiffon slip dress that effectively skimmed the slight thickening of her waistline and ended just above her knee, teamed with kitten-heeled white pumps and a matching purse, she descended the glass staircase into the hall, where Jake was waiting.

'A punctual woman.' Jake walked towards her and stopped at her side. 'And a very attractive one,' he complimented, subjecting her to a blatant masculine appraisal that made her tummy knot with tension. She hoped it was tension and nothing more primitive.

'If I have to see your doctor, can we go?' she said edgily.

'Sure. Take this.' He handed her a baguette stuffed full of meat and wrapped in cling film. Then a strong hand spread across her back and ushered her out into the brilliant morning sun.

A black limousine was waiting, and a man she had never seen before was holding open the rear door. Jake said something in rapid-fire Italian and the driver responded, and gave Charlie a long assessing look.

'Charlotte, *cara*, this is Marco.' Jake made the introduction, and Charlie politely shook the man's hand—a hand that was the size of a gorilla's. 'He will take care of you when Tomas is not available.'

'I am perfectly capable of taking care of myself. I don't need a minder.' She shot Jake a fulminating glance.

'Humour me, hmm?' His hand at her waist urged her into the rear seat of the car and he slid in beside her. 'And eat.'

At least it gave her something to do instead of having to talk to Jake, and surprisingly the sandwich was quite good.

The consultant gynaecologist, Dr Bruno, whom Jake took her to see was a small, friendly old man with twinkling eyes. He spoke fluent English and Charlie liked him on sight. He told her he had known Jake for years, from the time his son Paulo and Jake were at school together. Jake was the godfather to Paulo's son and daughter, his much-loved only grandchildren.

But she did not like him quite so much when the examination was over and Jake proceeded to question him on her and the baby's state of health, and he answered in a great deal of detail Charlie could have done without.

'Will you shut up?' Charlie hissed in exasperation and embarrassment as the older man turned to his desk to extract some booklets on pregnancy. 'It has nothing to do with you.'

'The child has everything to do with me,' Jake commented with a sardonic lift of an ebony brow, and continued his conversation with Dr Bruno in Italian, which did nothing for Charlie's temper. At least before she'd known what they were saying, but now she had no idea.

She heaved a sigh of relief when she finally stepped onto the pavement again, but her relief was short-lived as Jake caught her hand and led her towards the limousine waiting by the kerb.

'I know you have a meeting, so I think I'll have a look around the town, do some shopping,' she said lightly, banking on the fact Jake would not argue with her on the busy pavement. She pulled her hand free.

A muscular arm wrapped around her shoulders and Jake, his strong face taut, studied her with dark serious eyes. 'My home is not your prison, Charlotte, and I don't believe you will leave. Dave was right—you are an all-or-nothing kind of woman, and with you and I it cannot be nothing, as we will always have our child between us. So I am banking on the *all* when you get over the argument we had last night. Go shopping if you like.' His dark head bent and he brushed his lips against her hair.

'Marco will take you—and before you object, it's to make sure you don't get lost. This is a big city and you don't know your way around.'

'That sounds like a jailer to me,' she said stiffly, but in her heart she knew Jake was right.

Scornful dark eyes skimmed over her mutinous face. 'I thought we had reached an understanding this morning, but obviously I was wrong. Think what you like, you will anyway. But Marco stays.' Turning, he walked down the street.

Charlie inwardly cringed at the scorn in his expression. It was painful to have to admit, but she no longer wanted to leave Jake. Knowing he had only married her because she was pregnant did not stop her loving him and she watched his departing figure with a mixture of anger and sorrow in her suddenly moist eyes.

She didn't go shopping. She went back to the house—whether she would one day think of it as home, she didn't know.

CHAPTER TEN

CHARLIE ate a breakfast of fruit and cereal in the kitchen with young Aldo and grinned at his excellent attempts to speak English. When he left for school her smile vanished. It was a sad reflection on her marriage that her best friend and the person she spent most time with was an eight-year-old boy. He finished school at one and after lunch they had taken to exploring the extensive grounds together. He had shown her his favourite place, a cave set in the cliffs at the rear of the house, and she had told him about the fun she had rock climbing at her home in England.

Restless and on edge, Charlie rose to her feet, and with a thank you to Marta she carried her cup of tea outside to the small patio tucked away around the back of the kitchen. A pergola shaded the area, the crimson bougainvillaea trailing over it giving Charlie the sense of privacy she needed, and she let the sweet morning air work its magic on her troubled mind.

A week…she had been married a week today, but her wedding day seemed a lifetime away. The woman who had stood in the gardens of the Lakeview Hotel convinced it was the happiest day of her life was no more. A cynical smile twisted her lush lips. Love's young dream was just that—a dream. It had taken Jake to show her the truth.

She never saw him during the day, and dinner was pretty much a silent affair, or a battleground. Jake tried to make conversation but she replied with icy politeness, or with a bitter sarcasm that was totally alien to her usual sunny nature, until, finally exasperated with her, he retired to his study to work, and she retired to bed.

They shared a bed, but she was beginning to think it was for appearance's sake only, to prevent gossip among the staff. Once or twice she had awakened in the night to find his arm around her, but they had never made love since the morning after their disastrous wedding night. It was painful to have to admit, but she missed the intimacy.

She could see no clear end to the emotional mess she had made of her life unless she learnt to accept her marriage on Jake's terms.

Probably thousands of couples lived in a loveless marriage for the sake of the children quite successfully. Would it be so bad?

Sighing, Charlie drained her cup of tea. It couldn't be any worse than what she had now, and it was her own fault. She could not forget the anger and hurt she felt, and it showed. Then there was her unborn child to think about—but worrying wasn't going to help either of them, and with another sigh she replaced the cup on the table and leant back in her chair. The silence had a therapeutic effect on her, and slowly she felt herself begin to relax, but that feeling did not last for long. A shadow fell across her face and she looked up to see Jake's tall frame leaning against a timber pillar of the pergola.

She was shocked. He came to bed late and was always gone when she woke up in the morning. But today was different—Jake was different, the cool control of the past week no longer evident. Instead his mouth was tight and she felt the vibration of his underlying anger across the space between them.

'Shouldn't you be out making millions?' she said sarcastically. 'Instead of disturbing my peace and quiet.'

'I'm flattered I disturb you, Charlotte, but don't worry, I am not stopping. I have no desire to spend any more time than I have to with a sulky, immature girl.' Then, surprisingly, in an uncontrolled gesture he ran a frustrated hand through his thick dark hair. 'What the hell is the matter with you?' he demanded harshly. 'This constant sniping that passes as conversation from you has to stop. Can't you lighten up occasionally, or don't you have a sense of humour any more?'

'My sense of humour is still intact, thank you.' Anger was her only defence, but her words lacked their usual force. 'But after discovering on my wedding night that my husband did not love me but married me out of a desire for revenge and the child I am carrying, it is hardly surprising humour deserts me around you.'

'Love,' he sneered. '*Dio*, you are great at throwing that word around like a talisman, but it seems a pretty poor emotion to me that can't forget the slightest misdeed. Not even a deed—a wayward thought is enough,' he added bitterly. 'Give me honour and respect any day.'

Taken aback by his outburst, Charlie tried to defend herself. 'At least I believe in love.'

'You probably have to cling to the illusion with a father like yours, who had no honour or respect for women, marriage or anything else,' he said scathingly.

She went pale as his harsh words sliced into her and she linked her hands together on the table to stop them shaking as she recognised there was some truth in what Jake said. With the exception of herself, her father had respected no one, not even himself. He had drunk, smoked and drugged himself to death by the age of forty-six. She drew in a long shuddering breath, finally forced to accept that her dad had loved her in his own way, and that way had included ignoring her for the first eleven years of her life and, if Jake was to be believed, lying about her to his lady friends. Not the perfect love she dreamed of, and maybe that was her problem—she had expected too much.

Jake bent over and grasped her chin so she was forced to look at him. 'You have told me countless times you love me, but what you really felt for me, *cara mia*, for the first time in your life, was a lust for sex.' His other hand curved around her breast. 'And you still do.'

'No.' Her voice faltered to a halt and her mouth ran dry. His dark, handsome face was so close she could feel the warmth of his breath on her skin, and she looked away quickly, but not fast enough to stop her stomach curling tightly, and her breast hardening beneath his hand.

Jake's wide mouth curved in a cynical smile and he straightened up. 'Who's lying now, Charlotte?' She went from white to red, and he laughed. 'Still blushing.'

'Oh, shut up.' Her frustration boiled over and she lifted her glass to throw it at him. He grasped her hand.

'That is more like the exuberant girl I first met.' He grinned. 'Instead of the sulky silent shrew of the past week.' Dragging her to her feet, he added quietly, 'We could have a good life together, all three of us.' He slanted a glance at her stomach. 'With a bit of goodwill on both sides.'

She opened her mouth to say, *Never*, and closed it again.

'Wise woman,' Jake murmured gruffly, and pulled her against his hard body. She saw her own need reflected in his dark eyes and relaxed as his mouth closed over hers in a kiss that was achingly tender. A whole week without the taste of his lips on hers was in her response, and when he finally released her she was left swaying and breathless.

'Your hair is a mess,' Jake commented as he brushed a lock of hair back behind her ear. 'But don't worry, we are dining out tonight, and my PA, Sophia, is waiting to meet you in the house. She has kindly offered to take you to town to shop, get your hair done, whatever you women do.' Slipping his hand in his pocket, he held out a wad of money and a credit card in her name. 'Take this.'

'I don't need your money.'

'I know, and I will never forgive myself for once suggesting otherwise. So take it to save my soul.'

'That's a bit extreme,' Charlie said with a chuckle and took the money.

'There now, that didn't hurt.' Raising one hand, he lightly tapped her cheek. 'You have finally found your smile again, Charlotte. There is hope for us yet.' Grasping her hand, he led her back through the kitchen and into the hall.

Charlie took one look at the small elegant brunette waiting in the hall and felt terrible again. The woman was immaculately clad in what was obviously a designer suit, and Charlie felt like a scruff in comparison in a simple yellow sundress. It didn't help that Jake smiled at the other woman and said something in Italian whereupon they both laughed, and then turned to look at her, still grinning.

'Charlotte, *cara*, this is Sophia, my right-hand woman, and I could not do without her.' Smiling down at the beautiful woman, he added, 'Sophia: my wife, Charlotte.'

Reluctantly Charlie moved forward and took the small hand the other woman held out to her. She said rather stiffly, 'How do you do?' and wondered just exactly how much Sophia did do for Jake. Did it include sharing his bed? But as the woman smiled at her Charlie was struck by the warmth and kindness in her eyes.

'I have to go,' Jake said. 'Tomas will drive, and Marco will accompany you to carry your purchases so you will be safe in Sophia's hands, Charlotte.'

'Safe or secured?' Charlie shot back automatically, and felt even worse as she watched a tide of dark colour flood up Jake's face as he moved towards her, and curved a hand around her neck. He was right: she was turning into a shrew.

'Both,' he murmured, his dark head swooping to capture her mouth in a deeply possessive kiss. Only when he felt her quivering response did he trail his lips to her throat, nuzzling her neck. 'Don't you dare try to make our private battle public ever again, or you will live to regret it,' he whispered in her ear before straightening up and smiling down at her. The humour did not reach his eyes. 'Let Sophia show you around, listen to her advice and try to enjoy yourself—hmm?' Swinging on his heel, he slammed out of the house.

'Phew.' Sophia wiped her brow with the back of her hand. 'Talk about sparks flying, and I thought my husband and I were bad.' She grinned up at Charlie. 'But you shouldn't be too hard on Jake. He is bound to be a bit overprotective with the woman he loves. Now let's hit the shops.'

Charlie replaced the receiver, a bittersweet smile on her face. Talking to Jeff had restored her spirits a little. It was good to know the hotel was running smoothly and was waiting for her when and if she returned. Even though it did mean lying to Jeff that her marriage was running just as smoothly. But all that was about to change, she hoped.

While bathing and dressing for dinner she had come to a decision: she was going to give their marriage a chance. She knew it was partially the result of Jake's passionate kisses this morning, but more than that—his derisory comment about a love that would not forgive the slightest misdeed or even thought had hit home.

Jake was late. He had told her to be ready by seven, and she had been waiting for over ten minutes already. She was nervous, and she strolled into the family sitting room—a misnomer if ever there was one, she thought wryly, glancing around the elegant lounge. Perfectly presented but soulless was a more accurate description, much like her marriage, and it was up to her to do something about it.

'Your trip was a success?' Jake leant back against the doorjamb, and noted the slight thrust of her chin, the cool expressive features as she faced him. He suppressed a faint smile at the sleek, upswept hairstyle that ended with a purposely contrived bunch of wild curls on the top of her head. Very elegant, very chic: the many facets of his lovely wife were a source of constant fascination to him, though he would never admit it. One minute, playing with young Aldo in shorts and shirt, she looked like a teenager.

He knew because every night he had studied the security videos of them exploring the grounds. Then in the evening, cool and reserved opposite him at the dinner table, or, best of all, curled up in his bed, her beautiful face relaxed and innocent in sleep. He could watch her for hours, had done…

His loins stirred and he shifted away from the door willing his wayward libido under control. No, now was not the time. Tonight he was hosting a dinner party in an exclusive country restaurant that had been hired privately for the evening. He had instructed Sophia to arrange the party a couple of days before his wedding. At the time he had thought it was a great idea, a second reception to introduce Charlotte to all his friends. He had hoped it would be a wonderful surprise for her; now he only hoped they got through the night without her obvious antagonism showing.

'If you call being trussed up like a dog's dinner a success, then yes,' Charlie said wryly. The dress was a brilliant blue, which matched her eyes, and had a scooped neck with very short sleeves whose sole function was to hold up the princess-line bodice because the back was virtually non-existent to her waist. Sophia had assured her that her tummy didn't show and the dress, which ended above her knee, was the height of fashion. She had also approved the three-inch stiletto-heeled sandals that accentuated the length of her legs.

'You are no dog, Charlotte.' Jake grinned, his dark eyes gleaming with male appreciation. 'Sophia has done a good job. You look exquisite, the epitome of sophisticated young woman. Now prove you can act like one. Bring me a whisky on the rocks, upstairs—I'm going to get changed.'

She was about to refuse, but as she studied his handsome face with its dark eyes set beneath hooded lids and the almost permanent tightness that seemed to have taken control of his chiselled mouth she realised he looked tired. 'Okay.'

Charlie poured the amber liquid over ice cubes, and, lifting the crystal glass, she rotated it in her hand, her mind prey to conflicting thoughts. Ordered to serve her master, or a much-needed pick-me-up for a hard-working husband? For the first time since her wedding night, she allowed compassion to cut through her fierce pride, and slowly made her way upstairs.

She walked into the bedroom, looked around, and was about to put the drink down as Jake walked in from the *en suite*.

She stifled a gasp and all she could do was look at him. Black hair sleeked back from his forehead accentuated his handsome features. His superbly muscled body was naked except for a precariously slung white towel around his lean hips shielding his essential masculinity.

Hastily she lifted her eyes but it was difficult to meet his gaze as she moved towards him. 'Your drink as ordered.' She held out the glass with a hand that shook slightly.

'You have surprised me,' Jake said with a husky chuckle, and took the glass from her outstretched hand. 'Thank you. I need this.'

'My pleasure.' She forced herself to look up, to meet his eyes before she fled. But the searching intensity of his dark gaze kept her motionless. Since this morning something had changed between them—Jake had changed. The air in the room was suddenly heavy with sexual tension. Charlie drew in a quivering breath. She could feel the swell of her breasts beneath the fabric of her gown, and hastily she tore her gaze from his.

Noting her reaction, Jake quirked his lips in the briefest of grins, immensely satisfied that she was not as immune to him as she tried to pretend. And though it was chauvinistic to admit as much, he was privately delighted that Charlotte's experience of men was limited to him, and he intended it to stay that way. With that thought in mind, Jake broke the vow he had made to himself, and allowed a wicked, sensual grin to break the handsome contours of his face. 'And it will be your pleasure later, *cara*.'

Charlie blushed scarlet and fled, sure she could hear his throaty laughter as she closed the door behind her.

Back in the family room, she eyed the drinks cabinet in something like desperation. Never had she felt more like a drink in her life, but with her pregnancy it wasn't an option. Dear heaven! This acting the happy wife was a lot more nerve-racking than she had bargained for. A couple of kisses this morning and a teasing smile this evening, and she was in danger of melting at his feet in a puddle and reverting to the stupid girl who had gazed at him in dumb adoration before she had found out what a ruthless devil he could be. That was not what she wanted at all, but an equal relationship built on mutual respect and trust.

'You dashed off before I could give you this.' Jake's deep drawl had her spinning around to face him.

Charlie's eyes flicked over his broad frame, taking in the dark dinner suit, the white silk shirt and black bow tie, and she struggled to control the sudden racing of her heart as he approached her.

Where is your pride, girl? she admonished herself with a defiant tilt of her head, but her blue eyes collided with gleaming black, and she made no protests as he stopped and one strong hand circled her throat.

'Exquisite though you are, the dress lacks something,' he declared softly, a finger and thumb sliding down to caress the delicate hollows at the edge of her neck, igniting a sensual heat in the pit of her stomach.

'Bare is beautiful, but I thought something to reflect your sparkle, Charlotte.' With his free hand he withdrew a handful of jewels from his pocket.

'I don't need—' she began stiffly.

'Quiet, *cara*. Indulge me, because I do need.' Deftly he fastened a magnificent sapphire and diamond pendant around her neck.

Charlie gasped and lifted her hand to touch the jewels but Jake caught it and slipped a matching bracelet on her wrist. 'I don't want…'

'You do want,' Jake drawled with dry mockery. 'But you don't want to admit as much.' And before she could grasp his meaning, he had lifted her hand and slipped an equally fabulous diamond and sapphire ring on the third finger of her left hand to rest snugly against her wedding band.

'There, that is better.' He cupped her shoulders, his dark eyes roving over her with obvious satisfaction. 'No one this evening will be in any doubt you are my much-adored wife.' He drew her against him to press a swift kiss on the tip of her nose. 'Come, we must leave now or our guests will think we have deserted them.'

Free from the mesmerising effect of his dark eyes, Charlie's first thought was to remove the jewellery.

'Don't even think about it,' Jake commanded, reading her mind.

'If you think you can buy me, forget it. I am not for sale,' Charlie snapped back.

'I realised that some time ago,' Jake said with a wry smile and, clasping her hand in his, he linked his long fingers through hers. Together they left the house and got into the waiting car.

'What did you mean, meet our guests?' She belatedly remembered his other comment, when Jake slid into the back seat of the limousine beside her. 'I thought we were going out for dinner.'

'And so we are.' As the car sped through the evening traffic towards Portofino Jake explained it was by way of being a wedding reception for his friends and business acquaintances who had not been able to make the original service in England.

The thought of being on display before all his friends filled her with trepidation and she didn't offer a word for the rest of the drive to the restaurant. But she was intensely aware of Jake at her side. She had been in a state of nervous tension all day, and his thigh brushing lightly against hers was not helping at all.

Charlie heaved a sigh of relief when the car stopped and she slid from the seat the moment the chauffeur opened the door. But her relief was short-lived as Jake took her arm and led her up the massive stone steps of an elegant old building that belonged to another era, and into a marble entrance hall.

It was almost eight when they entered the dining room, and Charlie's eyes widened in shock as a trio of musicians stationed on a raised dais in one corner of the room immediately struck up with 'Here Comes the Bride', followed by an almighty cheer from all the assembled guests.

Blushing furiously, she was grateful of Jake's supporting arm as he introduced her to the elderly couple that stepped forward to meet them. They were his foster-parents, Mr and Mrs Lasio, and, seeing them hug Jake and then smile at her, she was struck by the underlying sadness in their eyes. It made her realise that Jake's reaction to the death of their daughter was not that extreme after all. And when they wished her a long and happy marriage with obvious sincerity, she felt incredibly guilty on her father's behalf.

'Don't worry. They don't know,' Jake murmured, accurately reading her thoughts, and, taking her arm, he led her to another group. The next half-hour was a blur of names and faces to Charlie as Jake introduced her to the hundred people that were his close friends and business colleagues.

She met Paulo Bruno, the doctor's son, and his wife Stephanie, and they did register with Charlie because within seconds of meeting them they were congratulating her on her marriage and her pregnancy.

Charlie coloured to the roots of her hair, and spared Jake a quick angry glance. She caught the faint gleam of amusement in his dark eyes, and realised he didn't give a damn who knew she was pregnant.

'This is Italy, *cara*,' he stated with a shrug of his broad shoulders. 'The prospect of a child is something to be celebrated at the earliest opportunity, not something to hide.' His dark eyes slid down to the barely perceptible swell of her tummy beneath the cleverly constructed slight A-line shape of her gown. 'But you do it well,' he added mockingly.

'You're impossible. And I need the bathroom,' she hissed, but not softly enough.

'I'll show you the way,' Stephanie offered. 'I can remember when I was in your condition and running to the loo all the time. It was hell.' Everyone laughed.

Having completed her ablutions, Charlie smiled at Stephanie. 'I suppose we have to re-join the fray.'

'Yes, unless you want Jake hammering on the door looking for you. I have never seen him in love before and it is amazing.' She gripped Charlie's hand. 'I'm so happy for you both, and especially for your baby. Jake will make a great father,' she said as they left the bathroom. 'And you don't want to believe all the stories you hear about the women he has supposedly known. Paulo told me they are vastly exaggerated—not that he has led the life of a monk, but Jake is a very moral man, old-fashioned in some ways. So you have nothing to worry about. He will make a marvellous husband and father.'

If Stephanie had sought to reassure Charlie, her information about all the women he was rumoured to have known had the opposite effect. Her determination to give their marriage a chance took a wobble—but face it, she told herself, she didn't have much of a choice.

'Charlotta, I thought you had got lost.' Jake's husky accented drawl, and the arm that curved around her waist, were a welcome relief from Stephanie's unwanted confidences, and her troubled thoughts. 'Dinner is about to be served,' he added and she made no demur as he led her back into the dining room.

The women were all elegantly dressed in the latest designer fashions, and Charlie said a private prayer of thanks to Sophia for guiding her in what to wear. As for the jewels, Jake had been right about that: she would have looked positively bare in this company where the diamonds on display had to equal a king's ransom—and not only on the women, she noted with an amused smile as Jake introduced her to a Signor Dotello. The diamond stud in the man's ear was the size of a gull's egg. His dress shirt was open almost to his waist and an enormous chain circled his neck, but that was not all: a massive diamond crucifix glittered against his deeply tanned chest.

'I believe that is what is called bling,' she murmured to Jake as the man left to take his place at one of the ten circular tables arranged around the periphery of the room, to leave space for dancing in the centre.

'Correct,' he said with a husky laugh. 'Dotello is a New York gems dealer and likes to show his wares.'

'Along with half his chest.'

'Not that you should not have noticed,' Jake declared possessively as he led her to the top table and saw her seated before joining her.

Jake deftly reacquainted her with their table companions. His foster-parents were next to him and then Sophia and her husband Gianni, followed by Paulo and his wife Stephanie who smiled at Charlie like an old friend.

The food was superb and the champagne and conversation flowed freely through half a dozen courses, except for the last couple at the table: Diego and a stunning Russian model called Lenka, who could not speak a word of any language but her own.

'Lenka is a typical Diego type,' Jake murmured to Charlie in a soft aside as Stephanie, having finished her sweet, tried to engage the model in conversation. 'Diego likes his women to be models, mobile and mute.'

'And of course you don't?' Charlie mocked with an elegant lift of a finely arched brow, remembering Melissa. Her blue eyes dimmed and she speared a solitary morsel of gateau left on her plate and popped it into her mouth.

'I have dated several, I can't deny it.' Jake settled back in his chair and regarded her with dark intent eyes. 'But my preference is for a beautiful English blonde, with a penchant for climbing, but not of the social variety, and maybe just a little bit too much mouth.' Leaning forward, he lifted a finger. 'Speaking of your delectable mouth, you have a crumb.' The pad of his index finger stroked the corner of her mouth and lingered.

'Come on, you two, less of the canoodling and lead the dancing,' Diego called with a laugh.

'Shall we?' Jake suggested smoothly as the band struck up the wedding waltz, and, rising to his feet, he took her hand and led her onto the dance floor.

With all his friends watching she could not disagree, but it struck her forcibly how little she really knew of Jake as he slid an arm around her, his hand splaying firmly across the centre of her back as he moved her in close to him. 'Do you realise I have never danced with you? I don't know if I can.'

'Trust me,' Jake murmured, grinning down at her. 'For a woman who moves like you in my bed, dancing is a given.' And he was right.

CHAPTER ELEVEN

THEY danced, Jake stroking his hand gently up Charlie's bare back, while the other caught her hand and held it tight to his chest. They circled the floor once to the applause of the crowd, and then other couples joined them.

'Thank God. I hate being the centre of attention,' Charlie murmured, tilting back her head to glance up at him.

'I thank God for you,' Jake murmured, his dark gaze intent on her upturned face.

Charlie's lips parted. The compliment was so unlike Jake she had trouble believing him, but there was something so convincing in his tone she couldn't help herself. Their eyes met and desire sharp as a rapier lanced between them. He raised her hand to his shoulder and left it there, to slide his own down to curve over her hip and urge her closer, one long leg edging between hers. She felt him stir against her and the familiar heat flowed through her.

Dear heaven, he felt so good, and though she knew he did not love her there was a sensual part of her that ached for his strength, the heat and power of his possession. She sank against the hard, lean length of him, her fingers instinctively linking behind his neck, her head resting on his shoulder as she gave herself up to the slow music and the sheer joy of being in his arms.

They were cocooned in a world of their own, and there was only the brush of thigh on thigh, hand on skin, the sensual stimulation of two bodies in perfect harmony as they moved to the slow, dreamy music.

Then the tempo changed to a loud disco beat.

Jake stopped, but held her close, his dark head dipping to hers. 'How long do you think before we can decently leave our own party?' he husked, his breath a warm caress against her cheek.

Mistily, Charlie glanced up at him, her blue eyes meshing with gleaming brown as he added with wry, self-deprecatory humour, 'Or, in my case, indecently.' The increased pressure of his hand on her bottom told her exactly what he meant.

She made no response; she simply gave him a slow sensual smile.

'That's it,' Jake growled. 'We're leaving.'

'We can't, the guests will be disappointed,' she murmured, not very convincingly, and saw his dark eyes flare and take on a devilish gleam.

'Not necessarily.' He grinned. 'Follow me.'

Five minutes later, after Jake had spoken to his foster-parents and a few of the guests, she found herself once more in the back of the limousine with Jake's arm draped around her shoulders.

'What on earth did you say to everyone to make them look at me so sympathetically?'

'I told them you felt faint and needed to lie down.'

'You what?' Charlie should have been furious, but instead her lips twitched in the beginnings of a smile. 'You liar.'

'Not exactly. *I* need to lie down.' His deep dark drawl fractured and his long fingers curved her neck. He tilted her head and his smouldering black eyes blazed down into hers. 'Quite desperately…with you.' His thumb stroked her nape, and then his mouth was brushing her lips slowly—oh, so slowly.

Her eyes fluttered shut, and his lie was suddenly the truth. She did feel faint. Faint with the myriad sensations flowing through her body, faint with love… Her mouth opened beneath his and a tiny moan sounded in her throat as the kiss deepened into a hungry, devouring force. He moved close, his hand raking up through her hair, sending the carefully contrived style into chaos as he angled her head. Her upper body was tight against him. The thought of resistance didn't enter her head, and when his hand slipped under the bodice of her dress, his fingers finding and teasing the pebble-like nipple, she shuddered, heat flowing through her like a river of fire. She wanted him, ached for him…

'*Dio!* What is it with you and cars?' Jake rasped, his dark head lifting, his hand slipping from her breast, his arms enfolding her to hug her tight. 'We have arrived, *cara*.' And it was only then Charlie realised the car had stopped.

In minutes they were naked on the bed, though Charlie had no clear memory of how they got there, and Jake was beside her, his dark eyes like molten jet sliding over her.

Her hair was loose, and he ran a hand through it, spreading the golden strands across the pillow in an almost reverent gesture before his head lowered and he took her mouth in a deep, open-mouthed kiss that went on and on.

For Charlie it was like coming home. She looped her arms around his shoulders, her fingers stroking through the silky hair of his head, and moaned her delight as she felt the caress of his hand on her breast. Heat flooded her veins, filling her body with sensual excitement as she arched against the teasing torment of his clever fingers. And she groaned out loud as he broke the kiss to dip his head and take the swollen peaks into his mouth, suckling first one and then the other. Her inner muscles clenched with need, desire lancing through her, making her hot and wet with arousal, and so very ready for him. Hungrily her hands roamed over him. He was all power and heat, and she gloried in the perfection of his body, and shuddered as he stroked and caressed her, kissing the slight swell of her stomach, and murmuring husky words of adoration to their unborn child. Then with tongue and hands he resumed his sensual quest, finding every sensitive pulse, tasting every intimate part of her, until she was a shaking, whimpering creature, lost to everything but the erotic pleasure he gave her.

Suddenly he reared back, and she stared in mute fascination at his arousal, a magnificent potent force between his thighs, wild with wanting. Then his hands gripped and lifted her and he was there where she ached for him to be, easing into her slowly, inch by perfect inch, his sensuous probing electrifying her until every nerve in her body was screaming for release.

She wound her arms around his neck, her head falling back, as with a powerful surge he slid in to the hilt. He repeated the movement, increasing the pace, his mouth finding her breast once more. She clawed at his back and sought his skin with her teeth, wanton in her need, and she cried out as her inner muscles spasmed around him in an explosion of pleasure.

Jake gave a deep, primitive growl and increased the pace and with one final thrust that seemed to touch her very womb his body shuddered in violent release. He fell back on the bed, taking her with him, and she lay sprawled on top of him, her body quivering and her head buried in the curve of his throat.

Jake's arms wrapped around her and he stroked her trembling body, gently, softly, until she sighed and lay still in his arms.

Tenderly he rolled her onto her back on the bed and leaned over her. '*Dio*, I needed you so much, *amore mia*,' he husked, bestowing a kiss upon her brow while his hand lazily traced the line of her shoulder and lower to cup her breast as if testing the weight, and then gently traced the swell of her stomach.

He needed her. It was music to her ears, and this time she did not object to the *amore mia* as a deep sense of peace flooded through her. After what they had just shared, she could let herself believe he meant it.

But she was rudely disillusioned a moment later as his hand was abruptly withdrawn and he stared down, his hooded lids lowering to shield his expression. 'But I should not have done it.'

'Leave the party, you mean?' she said softly, a smile playing around her mouth as she lazily lifted her hand to his square jaw. 'I'm sure no one will mind.' Her fingers caressed his slightly roughened chin. 'I know I don't.' She raised languorous blue eyes to his, and for a moment she saw some deep emotion in his dark gaze.

'Maybe not. But that isn't what I meant.' He placed a hand on her stomach. 'I couldn't bear it if I hurt our baby.'

'There's no fear of that. They are tough little beggars.'

'And you would know? You have had one before?' he mocked gently.

'No, but then neither have you,' she mocked back, tracing the line of his high cheekbone and up to his temple, the pad of her finger resting on the tiny pulse that beat there.

'I almost did once,' Jake murmured.

Her eyes widened on his and the anguish she saw in the swirling black depths had her hand falling from his face in shock. 'But… you…how?' she stammered. She felt the sudden tension in his long body pressed against hers, and heard it in his deep voice as he began to speak.

'I was young and careless, and five months into a not-really-serious relationship when my girlfriend told me she was pregnant. Naturally I offered to marry her. I bought her the engagement ring she wanted, and gave her the money she demanded to arrange the wedding, but when she realised I ploughed most of my money into building up my business and was not as wealthy as she thought, my fiancée spent the money on a holiday and an abortion instead of the wedding.'

'Oh, my God. That is appalling,' Charlie exclaimed, her hands involuntarily stroking his chest in a gesture of comfort. She could feel his pain as if it were her own, hear it in his voice.

'What is truly appalling,' Jake rasped, 'is the knowledge I paid to kill my own child.'

'No, you can't believe that. It wasn't your fault,' she told him. His hand pressed lightly on her stomach, but his mouth hardened as she watched.

'We are all responsible for our own actions, Charlotte, and the effect they have on those around us. She was my fiancée, not for any great love I felt for her, but out of necessity, and I should have known better than to trust her. But I learnt from it. I have never made the mistake of trusting a woman again.'

Her heart ached for him. He was such a proud man—what it must have done to him to know the woman in his life could betray him so abominably… With her new-found knowledge, she realised why he had so little trust in her sex. After what had happened to him, he had a right to be cynical. 'But not every woman is like your ex-fiancée, and you can't possibly want to live your life without trust,' she said softly.

Jake rolled onto his back. 'I've managed perfectly okay so far,' he said, pulling her into the curve of his arm. 'Forget about what I said. You have the damnable ability to make me reveal more than is good for either of us.'

Charlie leant up on one elbow. He looked so self-contained and devastatingly attractive that she felt anger mounting inside her. 'How can you say that, when it was that attitude that had you ranting and raving at me about money and proof when you discovered I was pregnant?' She paused as it hit her forcibly: Jake's insistence on marriage had not been solely about her baby, but the one he had lost. She remembered the expression on his face when she had wildly threatened to slit her belly open, convinced he wanted her to have a termination. How wrong had she been!

'That was why you insisted on marrying me. You had lost one child and were going to make sure it didn't happen again.'

'Charlotte,' he said tersely and the familiar shuttered look was back in his dark eyes. 'Does it matter why? We are married and I will support and protect you and our child.'

'The same way you protect yourself,' she said more scathingly than she intended. 'Blanking out anyone who tries to get close to you with a wall of ice around your true feelings. That's no way to live.'

He rose abruptly, and his narrowed glance held hers as he methodically picked up his robe and slipped it on. 'It sure as hell beats having to listen to your psychobabble in the middle of the night. I have to leave for Japan in the morning and I need to get some sleep. The bed next door will do me just fine.' And he turned on his heel and left.

She shivered, cold with the kind of heart-rending chill that came with rejection, and as she watched his back moisture filled her eyes. The euphoria she had felt in his arms was replaced by a growing certainty that Jake would never let himself see her as anything but the mother of his child, and a convenient lay when his overactive libido got the better of him.

Charlie brushed the tears from her cheeks, disgusted with herself for being such a fool as to love a man who didn't know the meaning of the word, and didn't want to. How many times was she going to let him use her, only to be slapped in the face with rejection afterwards? She deserved better than that.

Face it, she told herself. Knowing the reasons why Jake kept such a close control on his feelings or lack of them, and why he was so cynical about her sex, had done her no good at all. Because Jake was perfectly happy the way he was. He wasn't prepared to listen and had walked away.

Feeling listless, Charlotte refused young Aldo's requests to play with him after lunch, and decided to take a siesta instead. She hadn't slept or eaten much since Jake's departure five days ago. He had called her every day but the conversations had been short and stilted and yesterday she had put the phone down on him. She could not be bothered to talk to him as a polite little wife. She had reached her limit. And she wasn't sure she cared any more.

She felt as if she were living in a deep fog, where there were no longer any clear lines to follow, any certainty or purpose in her life, except for the baby she carried. She had been a woman of action, but she now seemed incapable of taking any, and she didn't like the woman she had become. Not bothering to remove her shorts and top, Charlie flopped down on the bed and closed her eyes, hoping that in sleep she could forget her troubles.

The sun was low in the sky when she awakened and, rising off the bed, she straightened her T-shirt and slipped her feet into white canvas loafers. She was thirsty and, running a hand through her dishevelled hair, she headed for the kitchen. A glass of juice would be good.

She filled a glass, drained it thirstily, and replaced the glass on the bench. Idly she looked around and wondered where everyone was. She strolled out onto the patio, and heard the sound of voices raised in what sounded like argument and the plaintive cry of some animal in distress. Walking around to the rear of the house, she glanced between the clutter of outbuildings to the rock garden and cliff beyond that provided a natural security barrier to the outside world, and her mouth fell open in shock.

Marta was at the entrance to Aldo's cave and crying her eyes out. Tomas was trying to comfort her, and Marco was speaking on a cell phone. The other security man from the gatehouse was surveying the cliff face.

Charlie heard the cry again before she reached the others, and as she lifted her head her heart turned over with shock. It wasn't an animal, but Aldo.

A couple of feet from the cave was a deep narrow fissure in the rock that widened out some twenty feet up and reached almost to the top of the cliff. Aldo had somehow managed to climb to where the gap widened and a narrow ledge protruded slightly. A colourful kite was visible on the ledge, no doubt Aldo's reason for the dangerous escapade. Unfortunately, with his small hands gripping the slight overhang and unable to haul himself up, he appeared to be stuck.

Tomas was struggling to climb up the fissure, but he was too large. Swiftly assessing the situation, Charlie did not hesitate. All three of the men were far too large to navigate the narrow chimney, and hastily she explained to Marco, who spoke the best English, what she was going to do. He tried to argue that the rescue team were on their way. But one glance at the perilous position of Aldo told Charlie they might be too late and she said as much, adding as reassurance, 'I am an expert rock climber and I free climb for fun. Trust me.'

And seconds later she began to climb. Looking up, she cried words of encouragement to Aldo. She had no doubt she could reach him—she had to. But she had grave doubts that she could get him back down safely. Her expert eye quickly concluded the ledge was her best hope. With luck she could lift him onto it and wait for the rescue service.

She quickly realised how Aldo had managed to get so far. The first fifteen feet were quite simple, providing a choice of finger and toe-holds. But she was a good deal larger than him and as she grazed her thigh, her knees and her back she cursed the fact she was wearing shorts and canvas shoes. As she got higher and the fissure widened again, she felt the sweat break out over her whole body as she struggled to find finger holds.

She paused for breath and thought of her unborn child, praying her exertions would not cause any harm. With one hand she sought the next hold, a tiny gap. It was big enough for Aldo's small fingers but she had to grasp it with her fingertips. Her knuckles white with the strain, she hauled herself up a little further. She chanced a brief glance down and they were all staring up at her, degrees of fear on their faces. She forced a confident smile to her lips for Marta's benefit, and then searched for the next hold, vaguely registering the sound of a racing car and sirens in the distance.

Her chest heaving, she looked up at Aldo. 'Keep still, stay still, Aldo. *Fermaressere,*' she called softly and hoped it was the right word—she didn't want him any more frightened than he already was. Taking a deep, ragged breath, her heart pounding fit to burst, she made one final effort. Legs and arms aching, she struggled on until she was alongside him.

'Charlie.' He stared at her, his dark eyes terrified and his little face streaked with tears.

'Don't move, it's all right. I'm here.' Using all the skill of years of training, she found toeholds either side of him, her own body covering his, and with her superior height and reach she curved one arm over the ledge, her long fingers searching to find the safest grip.

This was the difficult part, Charlie knew. She could simply hang there and wait for the rescue service—but if he panicked and let go, would her body take the weight? She doubted that would work, because any sudden movement on Aldo's part would probably dislodge her. The alternative was to tighten her grip on the ledge with one hand and hope to push him up and onto the ledge taking his weight at her own time.

Quietly she spoke to him, telling him to be brave, to stay calm and do exactly as she said, and prayed he understood.

Jake swore violently as he gunned the Ferrari through the wide-open security gates. What the hell was the point of paying for security if they left the damn gates wide open? Someone would pay for this, he thought savagely as he stopped the car with a spin of wheels outside the house. He didn't actually know what he was doing back in Italy when he had meetings lined up in Japan. But ever since yesterday, when Charlotte had quietly put the phone down on him, he had had an irrational need to see her again. Charlotte was feisty and sometimes furious, but never apathetic. Something was definitely wrong. He had ordered the jet and flown straight back to Italy, and now as he marched up the steps he was sure of it.

The great double doors were wide open. *Dio! Please, no, Charlotte,* he prayed as he stormed through the house calling her name. Run away, kidnapped or worse—he didn't know; he just knew he had to have her back.

Pain squeezed his chest. How could he have been so stupid? He, Jake d'Amato, head of an international company and renowned for his business acumen, his ability to make the right decisions, his rapier-like intelligence, hadn't been able to protect his wife of barely two weeks.

Entering the kitchen, he saw the open exit door, and walked back outside and around to the back of the house. He saw Marco and the security guard staring at the cliff through a red haze of rage and strode purposefully towards them.

'What the hell do you think you are doing?' he roared at Marco, and froze when they pointed to the cliff, with a gesture of silence.

As if in slow motion he glanced up and the sight that met his eyes made the blood freeze in his veins. Charlotte, his Charlotte, was suspended halfway up the cliff. He dashed to the base of the cliff, scrabbled for a handhold, anything. But strong hands hauled him back telling him it was useless—he was too big and too late, the signora was almost there, and he had to be quiet.

Wild-eyed he looked at them and back at Charlotte. He opened his mouth to yell he would kill her for being so stupid, and closed it again as it struck him like a knife in the gut that she was in grave danger of doing that for herself.

'No. *Dio,* no,' he groaned and watched, his heart in his throat, as her lithe body moved closer to the young boy. He saw her straddle him and her fingers grip the ledge. He saw her hesitate and then her toes sought a firmer hold and in that moment he guessed what she was going to do. He wanted to scream and yell at her not to be so foolish, and, God help him, he didn't care if Aldo made it; all he cared about was Charlotte.

He didn't hear the sirens; he was deaf and blind to everything in the world except Charlotte. For the first time in his adult life he was utterly powerless. Neither his strength nor his wealth could do anything about the tableau unfolding before his eyes. He saw her slender figure tauten and the breath stopped in his lungs as she let go with one hand and reached an arm around the young boy's waist. Ashen-faced, he watched. He felt the strain, the agony she must be feeling with every cell in his body, and he saw her with superhuman strength haul them both onto the ledge.

But it wasn't over yet. Suddenly he was aware of the police cars and the specialist fire appliance, the men all around him, and furiously he berated everyone in sight for their tardiness while scarcely taking his eyes off the ledge.

When it was decided the fire crane was the safest option, he demanded to be the one to go up in the cradle.

'No, sir,' the fire chief told him. 'Only an experienced operative is allowed—'

Jake didn't wait to hear the rest, and moved impetuously forward. A bunch of officers grabbed him. He lashed out wildly and managed to throw them off, but he was too late. The cradle with a fireman on board was winging skyward.

Cold terror gripped him, and he stood frozen to the spot as the rescue cradle was inched higher and higher.

Charlotte lay back on the hard rock fighting to breathe, her arm firmly around Aldo. She felt him squirm and cry. 'No, don't move,' she rasped, and tucked him gingerly into the curve of her shoulder, closed her eyes, and said a quiet prayer of thanks.

When she opened them she gave a sigh of relief. A metal cradle with a man on board was gingerly edging towards the ledge. Aldo moved and she tightened her hold on him.

'But I want my kite,' Aldo objected. 'The string broke,' he said with the simplicity of youth and she had to smile at the irony of it as the kite did a graceful dive off the ledge.

Still smiling, she commanded the man in the cradle, 'Take Aldo first,' slipping into the role of rescuer as she had done countless times before, and easing the little boy up into the officer's waiting arms. Then with Aldo clinging safely to the officer's leg, Charlie was hoisted on board.

The descent to the ground was accomplished in seconds, and as the cradle locked back onto the appliance a mighty cheer went up—*'Brava Charlotta,'* and much in the same vein she did not understand as she stepped back onto firm ground.

The first person she saw was Jake dressed in his usual garb of elegant suit, but with his tie loosened, and she thought she was hallucinating. 'Jake! What are you doing here?' And she smiled, more from relief at the successful completion of the rescue than any great desire to see her husband.

Fury roared through Jake. She was wearing shorts and a skimpy top, her hair was falling around her shoulders, her arms were scratched and her knee was bleeding, and she was smiling. She was actually smiling as if she had been for a damned walk in the park, and she had calmly asked him what he was doing here. He was damn near dying with fright for her and she… 'Shut up, Charlotte, just shut up!' he growled and took her in his arms and held her close to his chest, a great shudder coursing through him.

Shocked, Charlie looked at him. She had been trained to remain cool in a crisis, but obviously Jake was not. His eyes were cold and angry, exactly as they had been the last time she had seen him. No change there, then. His arms tightened in a deathlike grip around her and she yelped and pushed back. 'Please, you're hurting me. I think I've scraped my back.'

'Scraped your back?' Jake's arms eased slightly, and he stared down at her, his black eyes leaping with violence. 'My God, woman, you're lucky you didn't break your neck! Are you stark staring mad?' His anger washed over her in ever-rising waves. 'What possessed you?

You're pregnant, for God's sake. Have you got a death wish or something?'

'Or something,' Charlie snapped back. 'Common human decency, something you know nothing about.' He could not have made it plainer it was only the baby he was worried about.

Jake reeled as if he had been struck, all the anger draining out of him. His passionate, beautiful Charlotte was looking at him with contempt in her magnificent blue eyes, and he deserved it. He had been yelling at her like a madman when what he should be doing was comforting her—loving her. Finally he recognised what in his arrogance and conceit he had tried to deny. He loved Charlotte. He opened his mouth to tell her so, but the moment was lost as chaos reigned.

Marta swept Aldo into her arms, crying her eyes out, and berating him at the same time, then, grabbing Charlie's hand, she kissed it and thanked her over and over again.

Charlie murmured something appropriate, embarrassed by all the fuss. Police and firemen crowded around her with congratulations coming from all sides, and all the time Jake was at her back, his hand resting lightly on her waist, his dark presence towering over her.

All the people, the heat, the noise were making her head spin. A camera flashed right in her face and Jake dived past her to grip the hapless photographer and tear the camera from his hands.

Charlie's legs wobbled and for the first time in her life she fainted.

CHAPTER TWELVE

SLOWLY Charlie opened her eyes, and realised she was lying on the bed in the master bedroom. Jake was leaning over her, his handsome face grey and drawn, his eyes burning like black coals beneath hooded lids.

'You're awake, thank God. How do you feel? Where does it hurt?' he demanded in a voice that was not quite steady, and grasped her hand as if his life depended on it. 'Are you all right?'

'Oh, please,' she sighed, trying to sit up, but Jake gently pushed her back down. 'I'm fine.' And surprisingly, she realised she was.

The fog that seemed to have numbed her brain for the past few days was gone. Climbing the cliff, doing what she knew she was good at, while taking all her energy and skill had paradoxically restored her strength—her belief in herself. She didn't need Jake's concern—she didn't need him—and she glanced up at him, for once unmoved. 'How is Aldo? Is he all right?'

'Aldo is fine, hardly a mark on him, and confined to his room for life if I had my way. It is you I am worried about.'

'No need, I'm okay, but what are you doing here?'

'I could ask you the same question,' Jake said curtly. 'Unconscious in bed and why? Because you decided to scale a cliff to rescue that little devil instead of waiting for the emergency services.' A muscle jerked at the side of his mouth. '*Dio*—when I saw you climbing up alongside Aldo…' He shook his head in disbelief. 'If I live to be a hundred I will never forget that image. I nearly went out of my mind. I was sure you were going to fall in a crumpled heap at my feet.'

'You wish,' she mocked, and pulled her hand from his. His concern was too little and too late, as far as she was concerned.

'This is not a game, not something to joke about,' he grated, the tension in every line of his body evident as he added, 'You are my wife, you are carrying my child, and you could have killed the pair of you.'

She would never do anything to harm her child, and she had been as careful as she could. But it wasn't in her nature when any child's life was threatened to stand by and do nothing when she knew she could help. That Jake could think otherwise showed exactly how little he knew her. She might have told him so, but Marta appeared with Dr Bruno and a nurse in tow, and Charlie was grateful for the interruption. She didn't want to see Jake, didn't want to argue with him.

She did her best to ignore Jake's brooding presence as Dr Bruno conducted a thorough examination and pronounced the baby fine, and allowed the nurse to treat her cuts and bruises. Then they congratulated her on her act of heroism, and, horrified, she learned she had appeared on the television news.

'But how?' she asked, sitting up in bed. 'I saw you grab the man's camera.' She addressed her comment to Jake but avoided looking at him directly.

'The police cars have video cameras, as does the fire service; they film all their rescues,' Jake informed her, scowling. 'You are now the lead story on the local news station. And given you're a very beautiful and wealthy woman and you climbed a cliff to rescue a young boy, you will probably be splattered all over the national news, if not international.'

Charlie went pale. 'Oh, my God.'

'In fact, they'll probably dig up your life history, and the house will be besieged by paparazzi—'

'Now, Jake,' Dr Bruno cut in. 'Don't upset your wife; she has had enough for one day. But she is a remarkably fit young woman and the baby is fine, so you have nothing to worry about.'

'Are you sure about that?' Jake queried. 'I think she should be in hospital. She might have hidden injuries. What about a full body scan?'

Charlie looked at him as if he had taken leave of his senses, but the intense expression on his handsome face told her he was serious.

'I am the doctor here, Jake, and I can assure you Charlotte is fine.'

'But she was unconscious,' Jake said. 'Surely she must stay in hospital one night at least.'

'*She* is the cat's mother,' Charlie said in exasperation, sick of the two men talking about her as if she weren't there. 'And I was not unconscious. I fainted. And I fainted because I had little breakfast and no lunch, and after all that exercise I'm starving.' She almost laughed out loud at the stunned expression on Jake's face.

'There you are.' Dr Bruno chuckled. 'When a patient wants food there is not much wrong. Get Marta to feed her. As for you, Charlotte, eat and rest and no more climbing, until after the baby is born.' Turning to Jake, he added, 'As for you, Jake, do try and take better care of your wife. I don't understand you young men of today. In my day a new husband would never have dreamt of leaving his wife alone such a short time after the wedding.'

Jake didn't say a word. He couldn't, because nothing occurred to him but the gut-wrenching knowledge that he had nearly lost her. Dr Bruno was right; he should have taken better care of her. He looked at Charlotte, and her beauty and the shining spirit in her blue eyes shamed him. And all he had done since she had come down the cliff was yell or scowl at her. How could she possibly know it was because he had been terrified at the thought of losing her—still was…?

When Marta bustled in and told him to keep out of the way, she would look after Charlotte, he let her. After the arrogant way he had behaved over the past few weeks he no longer felt he had the right to object. It would be amazing if Charlotte even spoke to him again, and as for loving him, as she had declared frequently in the past—no chance.

Bathed, changed and tucked up in bed, Charlie had eaten a plate of delicious home-made lasagne and a huge wedge of chocolate gateau. Replete and tired, she refused Marta's offer of cheese.

'No, Marta, truly I don't want anything else, only to sleep,' she said gently. 'You go and look after Aldo. I'm fine.' She suffered Marta's thanks for about the thousandth time before Marta finally left.

She lay back against the pillows. It had been a traumatic day, but it had helped her clarify her thoughts on her marriage. She was going back home to England, whether Jake liked it or not, and when she saw him she would tell him so. But not tonight. She was tired. She let her eyelids droop, and was floating on the hazy edge of sleep when she heard the door close.

It was Jake, but he looked like something the cat had dragged in. His black hair was wildly dishevelled, as though he had been running his fingers through it. He had shed his jacket and tie and his shirt was open to the last button. His handsome face tightly drawn, he walked across to her and sat down on the side of the bed.

'What do you want? I was trying to sleep.' His dark brooding gaze roamed slowly over her, lingering on the gauze bandage on her arm, his mouth tightening. It was a warm summer night and she was only wearing a slip of a nightdress. The cover was draped around her middle, and Charlie gathered the sheet closer about her, feeling absurdly nervous as the silence lengthened.

'Aren't you supposed to be in Japan?' She raised her chin, determined not to let him intimidate her ever again.

'Yes, but my wife hung up on me, and, hard as it may be for you to believe, I was worried about you.' He reached for her hand and grasped it in his. She tried to pull free, but he tightened his grip. 'No, please, hear me out.' There was a look of determination in his eyes, but also an uncertainty about him she had never seen before. 'I did a lot of thinking on the flight over here, and I realised, in the short time we have been together, I have not been totally honest with you because I have not been honest with myself.'

Charlie was pretty certain she knew what he was going to say next and didn't give him the chance. 'You have no need to explain. I know,' she said woodenly. 'Our marriage was a mistake, and we both know it. It was always the baby you wanted and not me. And don't bother denying it.'

'It was never—' Jake began, but she lifted her hand to silence him.

'No, let me finish. I thought for a little while I could live with a marriage solely for the child, but I realised I can't. I'm going back to England.'

'Charlotte, I am—' She cut him off again.

'But don't worry, Jake, I won't deprive you of your child. We are both mature adults, I'm sure we can come to some amicable access agreement.'

'Amicable agreement?' His dark eyes flared, all trace of uncertainty gone. 'I don't want an amicable agreement!' he growled, once more his arrogant, demanding self. 'What I want is you, and I am trying to tell you I love you, damn it!'

'Oh, yes?' Charlie sneered, not believing him for a moment.

Jake's eyes bored into hers, dark and unfathomable, and a tiny muscle clenched at the edge of his jaw as he attempted to remain in control. 'I do love you, Charlotte. I think I have from the moment I saw you, but I told myself I didn't believe in love.'

'But now you do. How convenient, when I have just told you I am going home.' She tried for sarcasm but her voice wobbled ever so slightly. He sounded so sincere.

'No, love is not convenient, Charlotte. I have learned that much over the weeks we have been together. It is an ache, a hunger, a need that is all consuming. I tried to tell myself you were no different from all the other women I had known. In my heart I knew you were, but I refused to face it,' he said, leaning closer and gently stroking a strand of hair back from her face.

'When I spoke to you yesterday you sounded different, detached, and when you hung up on me—for the first time in my life, I was afraid. I ordered the jet and came straight back, but even then I was not ready to admit I loved you, because I did not fully understand what loving you meant.' He squeezed her hand so tight Charlie almost cried out. 'And then I saw the open gates, the empty house, and the horror scenarios that ran through my mind terrified me. I thought you had gone or been kidnapped, killed, and it was the worst moment of my life, but two minutes later I realised it wasn't when I lifted my eyes and saw you climbing that cliff.'

He was pale, Charlie noticed, but otherwise seemed to be maintaining a tight control. She sensed he was genuinely concerned—but then why wouldn't he be? She was carrying his child. 'You were probably relieved I wasn't kidnapped.' She shrugged, dismissing his fear. 'Think of the money I saved you,' she added nastily.

Jake stared at her, his eyes violent with some inner emotion of such magnitude that it took him a few seconds to successfully mask his expression. 'You think that badly of me?' His voice was bleak and his strong face clenched taut. 'Then you can leave when you like. There is nothing more to be said.' He turned to walk away.

Charlie suddenly saw red. He was doing it again, blanking her out. But this time they hadn't made love, but worse—he had said he loved her.

'Yes, there damn well is!' she shouted. 'You thought that badly of *me*, remember? A selfish greedy bitch selling her father's paintings for gain. Not so nice when the shoe is on the other foot, is it?' she snarled.

He spun around, his eyes hard as polished jet. 'I never said that, you did.'

'But you thought it,' she lashed back, and he did not attempt to contradict her. 'Well, let me tell you, Mr High and Mighty, all the money from my dad's art is going to the earthquake relief fund. With the agreement of Jess, the only one of his models I met. And as for *selfishly* refusing to meet your sister, that was my father's idea. I caught him once with Jess and, like most womanising men, I believe—and you should know,' she snapped, her blue eyes flashing fire, 'he was incredibly strict when it came to his own daughter. He didn't want me to meet his women, and whatever tales he told Anna had absolutely nothing to do with me. In fact, you're just like him, over-protective of your sister, and you'll be just as bad with your own child. So you know what? I'm glad I'm leaving. You're nothing but a workaholic, money-mad megalomaniac. And I hate you.'

Charlie swayed back against the pillows as reaction at the day's events and regrets for what could have been hit her badly. She placed a protective hand on her stomach and blinked back the tears that threatened.

For several seconds Jake stared back at her in shock. He felt about two inches tall. He could not deny he had once thought her capable of greed and selfishness and hadn't cared. At the beginning he had been content to have a willing Charlotte in his bed. She was right; he was everything she said he was, and more. He was a coward too, because he had never had the nerve to tell her how he really felt until she had almost killed herself. He was useless at this love thing, he thought, momentarily defeated. Then he saw her protective gesture and the tears she was trying so valiantly to hide, and he almost fell apart. But not quite. Instead he did the one thing he knew he was good at. He strode forward and sat down on the bed.

'You still here?' Charlie tried for sarcasm, but her voice wobbled.

'I am not going anywhere,' Jake said, and just snatched her into his arms.

'No? Well, I am.' She was leaving him, but somehow, held close in his arms, Charlie was suddenly too exhausted to fight him.

'No, you are not,' Jake muttered, and claimed her mouth with a gentle, possessive pressure. 'I am everything you say I am, but I love you, Charlotte.' His hand cupped her chin and she was unable to move. 'I am not very good at this, because I have never loved anyone before.' His mouth moved as soft as thistle-down to her eyes, and briefly brushed her lids. 'But I can't bear to see you cry, I can't bear to see you hurt. I can't bear to see you in danger,' he told her forcibly. '*Dio!* I love you so much I can't, I won't, let you go.'

She could only look at him. There could be no doubt he meant every word. It was there in the depth of his dark eyes, the husky determination in his voice, his touch as he brushed away a stray tear from her cheek, and carefully tucked an errant strand of hair behind her ear.

Hope and joy ignited inside her and heat washed through her veins, washing away her fears. Her blue eyes widened in wonder on his.

'I love everything about you,' he murmured softly. 'Though no woman has ever confused and frustrated me so utterly as you have.' His lips curved in a wry smile. 'Nor hurt me as much.'

'Hurt you?' Charlie asked. 'I didn't think that was possible.' But she saw the vulnerability in his dark gaze and was shocked.

'Oh, it is, I assure you,' he said, and then pushed her back against the pillows, his hard body pinning her down, and claimed her mouth with all the fierce passion of his arrogant nature. And she sighed against his lips, and pressed closer.

Jake lifted his head. 'I wanted you so much, Charlotte, but on our wedding day—' His eyes darkened but, as if compelled to talk, he carried on. '*Dio*, I listened to Dave telling me what you did, and felt ashamed I had not known. I glanced across and saw you so brave and so beautiful and thought I was the luckiest man on earth.

'And on our wedding night I needed you, ached for you so badly. I could not believe it when you mentioned Anna and the painting. And if Diego had been there I would have flattened him on the spot for putting the idea in your mind. I had long since given up any idea of revenge—it was a spur-of-the-moment, stupid idea in the first place. And I wanted nothing to spoil our night though even then I could not admit why.'

Charlie's lips parted in a soft, tremulous smile. 'Diego's revelation gave me a bit of a shock,' she murmured, lifting a hand to weave it through his soft black hair, and saw the expression on the face only inches from hers become slightly hooded.

'Not as shocked as I was when you mentioned the portrait in the bedroom, at the very moment I held you in my arms and kissed you. You have no idea how much it hurt me to see the doubt, the lack of trust in your eyes. I was furious and I lashed out at you.'

'You said you married me only for the baby,' Charlotte reminded him, but the hope in her heart was growing.

'I lied. I didn't marry you because you were pregnant. I didn't marry you for any other reason than I had to because I needed you and only you,' Jake said quietly, and brushed his finger across her cheek and round the contours of her lips. 'The baby is a marvellous bonus. But I was angry with you because it was my own guilt I could not face. Not only thinking badly of you but, if I am honest, because of Anna. You were wrong earlier when you said I was like your father and would be fiercely protective of any child. I never protected my child who was aborted, and I never protected Anna the way a real brother should. I never paid her enough attention—a lunch occasionally, and that was it. I had no right to be angry with you or your father. Anna was a grown woman and made her own mistakes. But I never learnt from mine. I never protected you, my wife, as Dr Bruno so succinctly pointed out.' To see her proud, indomitable husband so chastened, so vulnerable was a shock to Charlie.

'But if you will just give me a second chance, Charlotte, I swear I will protect you and our child with my life. You are the love I never thought existed,' he said huskily. 'And I want you so much.' He groaned, his eyes darkening as his gaze flickered over where the sheet had slipped and exposed the soft curve of her breasts barely covered by her satin nightgown, and then he fastened his mouth on hers in a kiss that was so piercingly sweet it melted her bones.

'You are so exquisite I can't think straight, let alone talk sensibly about anything, but, please, just say you will stay,' Jake pleaded. 'You said you loved me once, let me try to persuade you to love me again.' With a smothered groan he began kissing her again, until she started to tremble with emotion.

'Jake...' she murmured, her hand splaying across his broad chest, feeling the heat of his satin-smooth skin, the tickle of body hair on her palms. But still she pushed him away, and it was the hardest thing she had ever done. 'Please, I need to know,' she faltered. 'I need to know you truly mean this. The very first time we made love,' she said in a rush as Jake tensed, his dark gaze fixed warily on her face as though expecting some knockout blow, 'you turned your back on me and walked away in anger. Why? Was it something I did or didn't do?' She had to know she wasn't opening herself up to get left again afterwards.

'Oh, *cara*.' He paused to take a brief, hard kiss that left her breathless. 'That wasn't your fault, it was mine. You made me angrier than I could ever remember being before. I felt quite savage simply looking at you, because I had just made love to you and I wanted you again so badly. I could not understand the totally overwhelming sensations I felt just kissing you. And to be brutally honest I was still reeling from the shock of discovering the portrait of

Anna. I'd only learned of its existence a few hours before I met you, and I felt terribly guilty. I could not understand myself. I had to walk away or reveal my desperation for you, and I was not prepared to do that.'

'You wanted me that badly.' Charlie was thrilled.

'Oh, yes, and I still do, always will,' he said huskily.

But she wasn't totally convinced. 'If that's true, then why after our wedding day, when we finally made love, did you never touch me again? I hardly saw you. You never came to bed until the early hours and when you did you made a jolly good job of ignoring me,' Charlie protested, his coolness still looming large in her mind. 'Then when we did make love after the party, you stormed off in anger again.'

'That bothered you, hmm?' And his smile had a hint of passion intermingled with a touch of humour. 'You wanted me to make love to you.'

'No—well, yes.' She was sure he was laughing at her.

'Ah, Charlott-a-a. You really will have to learn my language.' He kissed her again, his tongue curling and probing her mouth, and she felt the breath catch in her throat when he lifted his head and smiled down at her, his dark eyes gleaming with love and emotion.

'It was all Dr Bruno's fault. He told me when you had your examination that the first few months were the most crucial of your pregnancy and it was better to refrain from sex. But after a week of abstinence I could not resist and once again I was angry with myself—not with you—for being so weak-willed. And when I told you about the abortion, and saw the compassion in your eyes, and heard your soft voice telling me I had to trust, I so wanted to lose myself in you. I had to leave. How could I endanger our child after what I had just told you?'

'Oh, Jake, that is an archaic idea,' Charlie said. 'Even I know that.'

'I wish you had told me. It would have saved me a lot of sleepless nights, and cold showers.' He hugged her to him, his breath warm against her cheek. 'Every night I would sit in the study and watch the security videos just to see you relaxed and playing with Aldo, and when I finally dared to slip into bed beside you I used to watch you sleep for hours. I knew then I loved you, but I was still fighting it. But today when you stepped out of that cradle with Aldo, and I yelled at you, I knew I could hide it no longer. I had so nearly lost you and life would not be worth living without you in my world. But then everyone mobbed you and I never got the chance.'

His confession was music to her ears. She looked at him and the love was there for her to see. She doubted anyone had ever seen him so vulnerable or ever would again. He was laying his heart on the line for her, and it moved her overwhelmingly. Wrapping her arms around him, she murmured, 'You have now, and I believe you. I have to because I love you, have done since the day we met.'

'At last.' Jake sighed and she saw the awe, the brilliant gleam of triumph in his smouldering dark eyes, as his head bent. 'You're mine—now, and for all eternity.' And his mouth captured hers in a deeply possessive kiss.

Charlie felt heat spreading through her as his mouth slid to her throat and the soft curve of her breast. Jake raised his head and looked at her, his eyes dark and questioning. She smiled and her arms lifted to tighten around his neck, her body arching beneath him. And with a fraught groan his control went and he showed her just how much she meant to him.

Later he held her possessively against his hard body, and studied her beautiful face, the sultry blue eyes, and her light golden skin on which the aftermath of loving had left a golden glow. 'Are you sure you're all right, Charlotte?'

'For a brilliant, intelligent man you really are a bit of a worrier,' Charlotte teased. 'Frightened because I climbed a few rocks—and as for believing Dr Bruno! For heaven's sake, the man himself is archaic.'

'Oh, Charlotte, you are priceless,' Jake said with a deep throaty laugh.

'You didn't always think that,' Charlotte said soberly. When she thought of how close she had come to leaving him, losing him…

'Forgive me, Charlotte, for every arrogant assumption, every harsh word,' he said softly. 'And I swear I will spend the rest of my life making it up to you and loving you.'

EPILOGUE

NINE months later Charlie peeped out at the beach from behind the corner of the villa. They had arrived on the Caribbean island last night. It was owned by a friend of Jake's who rented out his fabulous villa to a few selected guests. Absolute privacy guaranteed.

A mischievous smile curved her lush mouth as she spotted Jake wearing a pair of old shorts and stretched out on a lounger, a long arm reaching over the side to rock the carefully shaded cradle where their daughter of three months, Samantha, slept. She was the apple of her father's eye. Jake was totally besotted with her. Once a cynic about women, he was devoted to the brown-eyed cherub.

Charlotte took a last surreptitious look around and strolled down the beach. Some sixth sense must have warned Jake because his dark head turned and he leapt to his feet, the look on his face priceless as she sashayed towards him.

'Give me your opinion.' She gave him a twirl, the grass skirt that hung low on her hips rustling as she moved, and a strategically draped garland of flowers around her neck protecting her modesty. Lifting her head, she met Jake's dark, stunned gaze. 'Is it me?'

Jake reached for her bare shoulders, and placed a possessive, hungry kiss on her smiling lips. 'Definitely you. Stunning and beautiful and better than I could ever have imagined,' he said huskily, and folded her in his arms and held her firmly against his chest. 'As is my deep abiding love for you, and the perfect daughter you have given me.' He kissed her again.

'From a day in Kew Gardens to a real paradise island.' Charlotte smiled. 'I never thought we would make it, but we have. All three of us,' she murmured, her blue eyes brilliant with happiness and love.

MILLS & BOON® PUBLISH EIGHT LARGE PRINT TITLES A MONTH. THESE ARE THE EIGHT TITLES FOR OCTOBER 2005

MARRIED BY ARRANGEMENT
Lynne Graham

PREGNANCY OF REVENGE
Jacqueline Baird

IN THE MILLIONAIRE'S POSSESSION
Sara Craven

THE ONE-NIGHT WIFE
Sandra Marton

THE ITALIAN'S RIGHTFUL BRIDE
Lucy Gordon

HUSBAND BY REQUEST
Rebecca Winters

CONTRACT TO MARRY
Nicola Marsh

THE MIRRABROOK MARRIAGE
Barbara Hannay

MILLS & BOON® PUBLISH EIGHT LARGE PRINT TITLES A MONTH. THESE ARE THE EIGHT TITLES FOR NOVEMBER 2005

BOUGHT: ONE BRIDE
Miranda Lee

HIS WEDDING RING OF REVENGE
Julia James

BLACKMAILED INTO MARRIAGE
Lucy Monroe

THE GREEK'S FORBIDDEN BRIDE
Cathy Williams

PREGNANT: FATHER NEEDED
Barbara McMahon

A NANNY FOR KEEPS
Liz Fielding

THE BRIDAL CHASE
Darcy Maguire

MARRIAGE LOST AND FOUND
Trish Wylie

1005 Rom